BLACK TIDES

BOOK ONE

CURSE OF THE BLOOD PEARL

BY
CANDACE OSMOND

GUARDIAN
Publishing

DEDICATION

To every reader who loves my pirates as much as I do.
Thank you.

SUMMARY
OF THE ORIGINAL SERIES

Once upon a time, in the 1600s, there lived a woman named Constance Cobham. Orphaned at a young age, she was taken in by The Keepers, a secret group of Gaelic witches who uphold the sanctity of time.

When Constance was young, she meddled with the laws of time travel and found herself washed hundreds of years ashore in the future. There she fell in love with a man named Arthur Sheppard, and together they had a baby girl, Dianna.

But the Keepers were furious with Constance and pulled her back to her own time, abandoning her beloved and the daughter she loved with all her heart and soul, and leaving them to assume she'd drowned. Broken and desperate, Constance begged the sirens to grant her one wish; a baby to fill the void in her heart.

But the sirens are wicked things and never give without a cost. They gave Constance an impossible task in exchange for her baby; retrieve a siren's heart from the men who stole it. But try as she might, Constance couldn't find the ship they sailed on because it was cursed, you see, by the sirens themselves and tethered to an island that didn't exist.

Although she failed her mission, the sirens granted her wish and gifted her a baby girl, Maria. The cost? The baby was soulless, and siren blood ran in her veins. Constance tried to love the child, but she was a cruel and murderous little thing, and eventually pushed her mother away.

Meanwhile, in the future, her first child Dianna was a woman now and mourned her father's sudden death. While going through his belongings, Dianna found an old ship in a bottle that, upon breaking, washed her back in time to 1707 Newfoundland, where she was taken prisoner aboard a pirate ship called The Devil's Heart, captained by the infamous Devil Eyed Barrett aka Henry.

Using her skills as a chef, Dianna won the crew's hearts and fell in love with the captain. Little did she know that her sister, Maria—the insane half-siren—had been trapped within the ship in a bottle, and upon breaking it, Dianna had set her free to wreak havoc on the seas again.

But Maria had another plan; find and kill her mother.

So, Dianna and the crew banded together to stop her evil sister and save the mother she thought had drowned at sea many years ago. Their ship encountered a massive storm on their tumultuous journey across the Atlantic, and Dianna went overboard. She washed up on a desert island and discovered a ghost ship trapped by a siren's curse. She befriended one of the crew, a man named Benjamin Cook, and together they broke the curse, setting them all free.

With the curse broken, Dianna was saved by her own crew, and they continued their mission to find her evil sister. There were losses along the way, but the band of misfits eventually won, so Dianna and Henry returned to the future to live happily ever after with their twin children, Audrey and Arthur.

And thus, our story begins.

CHAPTER ONE

ACE

Not many people know what it's like to die.

But I did.

The thought held me as I let the cold, relentless depths of the sea take me once again, dragging me under as I fell weightlessly through the abyss, just as I did every night, and my arms drifted outward while I waited for the inevitable end to come. I knew it was in the darkness below, just beyond my fingertips.

It was always there.

The call of death, the sweet promise of an end to this empty nightmare. I've grown tired of waiting for it. Night after night, the broken memories of my past weighed me down and lulled me to sleep as I slipped into the same tangible dream of nothingness.

I sank into the sea like a leaf falling to the ground–knowing I'd never reach it–and the cold darkness slowly rose to meet me as I waited to wake up.

But this time was different.

My slowing heartbeat thwomped in my ears, picking up speed as the black pit grew closer, and the unrelenting chill of the sea seeped into my bones. I dragged my arm through the water, straining to touch my fingertip to the darkness, but a strange white light suddenly sparked to life in its center.

This was new.

Curious, my mind dragged, and the light grew bigger and brighter, blinding me. This was not the death I was promised. I tried to swim away, back to the unreachable surface, but the ocean was like glue, and I couldn't go back, only forward to the unfamiliar light.

Slowly, I reached down, and as my fingertip breached the edge of the expanding light, the dream shattered all around me. The enraged sea screamed in my ears as it gathered in a whirlwind. The water receded, and my bare feet planted firmly on a smooth rock as I stood in the center of the tornado, aghast at the sight before me. I'd had this crippling nightmare every night since I was four, and never did it end like this.

The light hovered above, blocking out the starless sky,

and my jaw hung as I stared up at it in wonder, just as the wild sea twirled into a spout and dove into my gaping mouth, forcing its way inside my body, filling every brimming inch of me until I gaged on it.

My back slammed into the rock, and I gasped for breath as I shot up in bed.

"Fuck," I breathed and ran my hand through sweaty white curls.

The early morning sun burst through my window blinds, casting a pattern of stripes across my bedroom. I grabbed the tepid water from my bedside and downed it as my phone vibrated against the glass top. A groan turned over in my chest when I glanced at the screen and saw six missed calls. One was from work.

Five were from my mother.

I swung my bare legs out of bed, relieved to be rid of the hot blanket, and stomped over to the kitchen for more water as I called my assistant.

"Ace!" Evelyn squealed from the other end. "Where are you? You're late."

After chugging another glass of water, I cleared my throat and wiped my mouth with the back of my hand. "See, that's the best part of owning the firm, Ev'. I make my own hours."

She laughed. "You're just lucky you have me."

"I know."

"Listen, I have a lead on a new project. Do you have time today to sit down?"

I rifled through my closet of mostly black garments. "I can't take on another client, Ev. You know how jam-packed I am. Are they willing to pre-book for…" I tossed my planner on the bed and flipped through the next couple of months. "Maybe late September?"

"Ace, I can take over a few of the small accounts," she replied, hardly able to contain the excitement in her voice. "You might change your mind once you see the project's details. Specifically, the budget."

"Fine. I'll be ready in half an hour."

"I'll send a car," she said and hung up.

I had my own car, but driving around downtown Edmonton during work hours was more work than it was worth, and parking was practically a mythical creature. So, I used a town car service during the week.

I settled on a black sleeveless jumper with wide legs. It was the dead of summer in Edmonton, but I couldn't sacrifice my signature black attire. Paired with my long platinum curls, skin that looked like it never saw the light of day, and eyes so brown they almost appeared to be one large black pupil, my signature style was my brand.

I have been the face of Ace Interiors for three years now. I had quickly grown from a newbie in the city to a well-respected interior designer catering to dozens of home builders and property investors. I specialized in urban living and restorations, but no one was currently restoring anything worthy of sinking my teeth into. So, I loaded my plate with condo developments and a few major house flips.

As expected, the town car pulled up at the front entrance to the condo complex I lived in, and I arrived at the office within twenty minutes. I greeted June at the front desk and passed Dawn in accounting with a simple nod. She hated being interrupted, so I rarely bothered her with trivial greetings and small talk. She respected my space as the boss, and I respected hers as the person who kept our small firm in check. I may be the captain, but she was an integral part of the engine.

As was Evelyn.

My assistant had been with me since day one when I was bidding on every job possible from my home office. She operated from my couch, and we built Ace Designs to be one of the best places in Edmonton to handle high-end design jobs.

I strode quickly for my office at the end of the downtown commercial loft, my chunky heels on the bamboo floors echoing off the distant walls. Evelyn scurried in behind me, fiery red hair falling out of the claw buckle she always wore, arms stacked with binders and papers. She shut the door behind us and sat down across from my desk.

"Okay, give me the low down on this project," I said as I fiddled with the Nespresso machine behind my desk.

"Projects, plural," she replied, opening a thick black portfolio. "Ace, this guy is a gold mine. He's a massive property investor and loves flipping old properties."

I sat down, my eyes wide with delight. "We love old properties."

She nodded with a grin. "That we do."

"So, what's the current job open for bids?" I spun halfway around in my chair and grabbed my steaming cup of coffee as Evelyn splayed papers and drawings on my desk. "He just took over that collection of abandoned airport hangars out by Leduc. He wants to turn the whole thing into a small luxury resort with a rustic vibe."

My heart quickened. "Say less," I said over the rim of my mug. "Okay, and what's this killer budget you mentioned?"

Evelyn's grinned spread as she slid another piece of paper across the desk's surface. I picked it up and scanned the words and numbers that filled it. My chest tightened.

My assistant cleared her throat and leaned back in the chair. "Told you."

"This…is nearly three times the fee we'd normally charge for a job like this."

"Let's throw our hats in, Ace."

I rocked back in my big leather chair, rereading the budget proposal and considering this project's scope alone. If we got it, it could open doors to all the other projects this guy has in the pipeline. I took another sip of my coffee, pretending to ignore how Evelyn practically bounced in her seat with anticipation.

I raised my gaze to her eager stare. "I'd need your help with the condos on Whyte."

She could barely contain herself. "Definitely."

"And you'd probably have to work a few nights."

She tipped her head to the side and gave me a look that said, *please*. "I'm a childless, single woman in my mid-twenties. I have all the time in the world."

I mirrored her grin. "Let's do this. Whip up some renderings for me to take. I'll call his office right now and arrange a meeting on-site. What's his name?"

Evelyn double-checked one of her many folders. "Uh, Cook. Benjamin Cook."

CHAPTER
TWO

According to his secretary, Mr. Cook didn't have an opening for another three days. And even then, she could only squeeze me in for a quick site meet. So, three days later, I drove down a long dirt road and pulled up to four old airport hangars from the late fifties.

I eyed the perfectly spaced properties; one giant hangar fronted by rolling doors embedded with old glass panels, two more simple warehouse-style buildings, and then one rather large Quonset. There was plenty of room for generous parking and even adding more buildings. I could already imagine what we could do with the place.

I stole a glance at the clock on my dashboard and

peered around the site, noting the dirty work trucks and heavy-duty equipment, no fancy cars fit for a millionaire. Mr. Cook was already ten minutes late.

Typical.

I waited another ten minutes before calling his office to double-check that the meeting was still on, and his secretary assured me that Mr. Cook never missed an appointment. With a sigh, I gathered up my tablet and tape, threw on a pair of sunglasses, and stepped out of the car. If this guy wouldn't show up, at least I could look around and verify some measurements.

After sizing up some vintage windows I hoped he planned to keep, footsteps sounded from behind me, heavy work boots that crunched against the dry dirt.

"Can I help you, miss?"

I stood and turned, unable to hide the smile on my face. He was a towering man with grungy clothes that clung to his broad, muscled construction-worker body. He removed his hard hat and tucked it under his arm as soft brown waves fell to his shoulders, the same color as the week-old beard that softened his rugged facial features. Toned from hard work and most likely emotionally unavailable?

He was just my type.

"Sorry, I was just taking some measurements while I waited for your boss," I told him. His brows pinched together as he sized me up from top to bottom. "It, uh, doesn't look like he's gonna show. Typical rich guys, working on their own time." He didn't share the nervous laugh I let out. "So, I'll head out after I take some pictures."

"You the new designer?"

I shook my head. "Not yet. I mean, I hope to be. I was supposed to discuss details with Mr. Cook here this afternoon."

The guy crossed his arms, flexing the corded muscle beneath his smooth, tanned skin, and leaned against the side of the building. "You don't even have the job, but you're spending your time taking measurements?"

"I'm a bit of a workaholic. I love what I do and like having as many details as possible when quoting a project."

"I hear the budget for this one is sky-high. Why bother?" His deep voice raked through me.

"Yeah, it's not the budget that attracted me to this one, though." He raised his brows in surprise. "I'm sort of an old property fanatic." I glanced at the dusty old windows admiringly. "I'd give anything to work on this."

"What's your name?" he asked.

I offered a hand. "They call me Ace. You?"

He had the grace to wipe his dirty hand on his pants before slipping it into mine and shaking firmly. "Ben Cook."

My blood stilled. "Wait…you mean…"

He gestured around us. "The pompous rich asshole who's late for the appointment? Yeah." He mockingly glanced at his wrist as if there were a watch there. "But looks like you're the one who's late, Ace." He threw me a wink and shoved from the wall.

I silently cursed the heat that rushed to my face, knowing very well how it clashed with the pallor tone of my skin. "I don't know what to say, Mr. Cook. I'm so embarrassed–"

"Please, call me Ben," he quickly amended and fished a Sharpie from his Carhartts. He grabbed my hand and popped the pen top off with his teeth before spitting it out. "Every other designer that came out here was only interested in one thing. The money. But not you."

My voice evaded me as I focused on how his massive, calloused hands held mine and dragged the wet tip of the Sharpie across the skin on the back. A number…no, an address.

"If you want the job, come by my home office this evening with a proposal and some ideas." He scooped the lid from the dirt and popped it back on before slipping the marker into his pocket. I stood there, speechless like an idiot, mouth gaping, and Ben gave me a wink as he turned and headed back inside the building with a chuckle.

***

Later that evening, I headed to the address Ben scribbled

on my hand, which I had quickly transferred to my tablet contacts. But after driving past Sir Wilfred Laurier Park twice, nothing but the river to my other side, I realized there were no residential properties around the address he gave. In fact, the address itself didn't exist.

Cursing, I pulled off to the side and drove down a small dirt road to park and call Ben's offices. As I neared the end of the road, the trees parted and opened up to a row of boat launches and one larger dock that led to a beautiful houseboat lit up with strings of twinkle lights. Even from inside the car, I could hear the soft tempo of music coming from the boat.

"You've got to be kidding me," I muttered, exiting the car.

As I stood and stared, I realized…this was the address Ben had given me.

"Ace!" he called from the deck, waving like a big idiot. "Late again? You really don't want this job, do you?"

I approached the dock. "Sorry, I didn't realize your home office was…floating."

Ben jumped off the side of his boat and landed on the dock with ease. "Don't like boats?" he asked as he walked toward me. "Ol' Gertie's solid, I promise."

Hugging my arms tight to my chest, my stomach clenched as I stared at the Fort Saskatchewan River, trying not to let images of my nightmares flood my mind. "No, I don't like water," I replied. "I…can't swim."

Without missing a beat, Ben held out one of his giant mitts and smiled so kindly that I couldn't help but breathe a sigh of relief. "I'll try not to throw you overboard, then."

For a big, tough, grizzly type of guy, he had a sort of softness about him, like a rugged, muscley teddy bear. Still, I hesitated. How do I tell this man I barely know that the ocean haunted me every night and I had a crippling fear of water?

Looking at the warm twinkle in his brown eyes, I knew I couldn't. I was safe here. So, my portfolio clutched in one hand, I slipped the other into his and let Ben help me cross the dock and board his boat. My palms grew sweaty, sliding against his, and my heart raced.

"Geez, you really are that scared of water?" he said, wiping his hand on his plain white t-shirt.

I took a couple deep breaths. "I…drowned when I was little. My parents saved me before it was too late, but I haven't been able to go near the water since."

"Well, in that case," he replied, opening the narrow door to the cabin. "Let's take this business inside, shall we?"

Everything in my body screamed for me to run and get as far away from the water as possible. But this man, this potential new client, waited for my response with a warm smile that crinkled the corners of his eyes, and something inside of me whispered, *you're safe.*

So, I took a deep breath and shrugged off the unwarranted fear. This was the Fort Saskatchewan River, for Pete's sake, not the big bad ocean. I nodded and stepped inside the cabin as Ben closed the door behind us. I immediately noted that it'd recently been renovated, and the ceilings heightened. Ben's head wouldn't have cleared it otherwise.

Scents of bacon and vanilla wafted across my nose, and I took a moment to admire the gorgeous interior. Walls covered in warm wood paneling, benches upholstered in worn leather, and a quaint cast iron wood stove in the corner. On one side, a modest set of birch cabinets held a kitchen sink and some storage, topped by a few rows of white open shelving that displayed a few dishes. The other side held a long, narrow desk covered in papers and books.

"Do you like it?" he asked from over my shoulder. So close I could feel his breath ruffle my hair.

I stepped away and turned to him with a smile. "It's gorgeous. You live here?"

"For now," Ben replied and sat at the desk. "It began as a passion project. The whole thing was barely holding together when I nabbed it at auction. I remodeled everything and had planned to sell it for a killer profit, but when I was done, I couldn't part with it."

I nodded, glancing around at the finer details. "I get it."

Ben seemed to love old marine trinkets, framed maps,

rusted tools, and weapons. But it worked with the blend of nautical touches like thick rope holding up shelves and brass fittings on everything.

"It's beautiful," I said, tearing my eyes away and realizing his had been on me the whole time. We'd only just met, we were strangers, but Ben seemed to look at me with a sense of recognition ever since we met. Or maybe it was something else. I cleared my throat and waggled my black leather portfolio. "Shall we?"

Ben cleared his throat. "Yes, of course. Have a seat." He quickly cleared some space on his desk.

I sat in the chair across from him and opened the portfolio to reveal my written plan for the old airport hangars. Evelyn had transferred the renderings to my tablet. So, I sifted through each perspective and idea with him for an hour. We discussed aesthetics, space, capacity, sourcing, timelines, and everything else under the sun. In the end, Ben sat back in his chair and blew out a long breath as he looked over the papers once more.

He scoffed in disbelief and tossed the sheets on the desk as he looked at me, eyes brimming with excitement. "I love it."

My chest filled with hope. "You do?"

"Yeah, it's the best proposal I've seen. You're visualizing exactly what I wanted." Ben stretched an arm across the table. "You're hired, Ace. Welcome aboard."

I gave it a firm shake. "Literally."

He laughed and stood from his chair. I noticed he kept a red mini fridge beside where he sat as he fetched two Coronas. He popped the tops off both and handed one to me.

"Celebrate?"

My rational brain screamed no. This wasn't professional, this wasn't me, and if it were wine or champagne that he offered, I probably would have refused. But a beer…it seemed so friendly. Especially coming from Ben.

I sighed and let my shoulders slump. "Sure, why not?" I pinched the cold neck between my fingers. It's been a while since I had a nice cold beer. Years, even.

Ben tipped his toward me, and I leaned forward to clink our bottle together. "To new beginnings."

I smiled. "To a shared love of all things old and rusty."

He laughed and brought the bottle to his lips, letting almost half the beer pour into his mouth. We chatted more about the project, and he told me bits and pieces of plans for future ideas he's been scoping out around Alberta, even a new lead on an abandoned beach house on Vancouver Island that he was seriously considering.

"A beach house?" I finished off the last mouthful of my third beer. "For personal use or flipping?"

"Not sure yet," Ben replied. "I love the sea, obviously." He gestured around the boat house. "Now that I'm done renovating Gertie, she needs a permanent home. If I had a beach property, I could add a dock and park her there."

"If you're interested in coastal investments, I know a ton in Newfoundland," I told him.

His eyes glistened with interest. "Newfoundland?"

"Yeah. Have you ever been?"

Ben almost seemed to recall a memory, his gaze distant and longing. But he shook his head. "Not in a very long time."

Wherever his mind had wandered, whatever memory he'd gotten lost in held him there for a little too long for comfort, and I cleared my throat as I stood from the chair, woozy from several Coronas. I braced a hand on the back of the seat and chuckled.

"I'm, uh, I'm gonna step outside for some air," I said, tossing my phone back in my purse after messaging for an Uber.

Ben's eyes slipped back into focus, and color flushed his cheeks as he scrambled to his feet. "Are you alright?" He slipped a hand under my elbow, his face wrought with concern.

"Yeah," I released an exasperated puff of air and wiped my forehead. "Just the damn Edmonton summer heat and one too many beers. I'm not a big drinker."

We stepped outside, and he led me to a little built-in bench that hugged around the edge of the deck. The twinkle lights overhead glimmered on the water with moonlight as the river gently lapped against the side of Gertie. The sounds of the city were far in the distance, muffled by the thicket of trees that lined the river. It was peaceful here as if time slowed down.

"So, did you overhaul Gertie all by yourself?" I asked, already feeling better as fresh air filled my lungs.

Ben shrugged and stretched out his tree-trunk long legs, crossing one sandaled foot over the other. "More or less. It quickly became a passion project, and I didn't want anyone else touching it. So, I worked on it in my spare time when I wasn't on another site or project."

"Do you always do laborer work on your projects?" I thought of how I easily mistook him for a general laborer earlier that day. His hands bore signs of hard work; callouses, scars, half-cleaned paint splatters he'd missed.

"Yeah, I can't help it." He scooted slightly closer to me, and I didn't move away. "I'm a hands-on guy, always have been." The cheeky look in his eye glistened as he winked at me.

I couldn't help but laugh; it was hard not to feel light around this guy. I glanced at my watch.

"You shouldn't drive," he noted. "Stay the night."

I feigned innocence with a clutch-my-pearls look. "My, Mr. Cook, you move fast."

He rolled his eyes. "No, lightweight. You've had three

too many beers to drive. I've got a nice couch you can crash on." He waggled his brows. "But my bed's also pretty comfy."

I playfully shoved at his shoulder. "Nice try." A car appeared, rolling down the dirt road, and stopped next to mine. I waved at the driver. "I called an Uber ten minutes ago. Thank you for the offer, but this *will* stay professional, Benjamin Cook."

"Ooh, I love how you say my name," he teased.

I stood and slipped my tablet inside my bag, giving him an exaggerated look under my lashes. "Goodbye, *Benjamin Cook*," I spoke his name slowly, annunciating every syllable, and he tossed his head back and capped both hands over his heart as if I shot him, eliciting another chuckle from me.

When I headed toward the exit, he stood, took two long strides, and offered to help me down to the dock.

"Milady."

I rolled my eyes.

"What? Is that not professional?"

I said final goodbyes and made my way to the waiting Uber thinking how it'd never be professional between us if he continued looking at me the way he did. But I couldn't give up this project and all the potential it brought. I'd just have to keep Ben in check.

And maybe myself.

CHAPTER THREE

Over the next few months, Ace Designs operated at full capacity, and happily so. I had the world's best team, and our small firm ran like a well-oiled machine. With Evelyn handling all the small accounts, I devoted my time to Ben and his never-ending projects. While most would feel monopolized by the client, I dove in head first and let the work consume me. I loved it.

Working closely with Ben didn't hurt, either. He was funny, charming, and so easygoing that I sometimes forgot my place and had to remind myself he was a client and not someone I'd known my whole life.

He'd show up at a job site or our meetings with gifts

each day. Chocolates, coffees and teas, and flowers. And, every single time, I'd set the gift aside and pass it off as nothing, as if it didn't impress me. Finally, after nearly a month of working together, he handed me a small bouquet of white flowers, and I called him on it.

"Ben, I told you, this is strictly a professional relationship. So, unless you bring gifts to everyone you work with, this must stop."

He just grinned like an idiot and agreed that I was right. The next day, he showed up at the job site with roses for every worker.

"I appreciate every talent and skill that works with me," he said coyly, handing me a white rose.

I accepted it, threading it through the coils of the notebook I carried around. His face was an open book, and the expression all day was that of triumph. Little did he know I'd filled vases around my office with every flower he'd already given me.

Since our original meeting, Ben had purchased several more old properties around Alberta and had me driving around to each one with him. It'd been weeks of road trips and diner food, overnights at hotels—not fancy ones that you'd expect most millionaires to book, but regular, everyday hotels.

One evening, in his suite, surrounded by open boxes of Chinese food and endless blueprints, he switched on the

T.V. and left an episode of Yellowstone playing as background noise while we worked. I'd made some passing comments about the ranch house and how I'd love to get my hands on a project like that.

The very next week, he brought me to a small ranch near the southern border and asked for my opinion. He bought it on the spot.

"Any plans for tonight?" Evelyn asked as she sat in my office and watched me dump dead flowers into the garbage.

"Just a glass of wine and a pile of supply orders to fill out. You?"

"I'm headed to a new club downtown with some friends," she replied as she slipped her arms through her jacket sleeves. "You should come. Take a break from working on Romeo's projects; you look like you haven't slept in weeks."

She wasn't wrong. The purple rims around my eyes had spread to the point of looking like overdone eyeliner, contrasting with my pale skin and ghostly loose curls. My nightmares of drowning had escalated, and I just chalked it up to spending so much time on Ben's houseboat.

I gave Evelyn an incredulous look, and she just rolled her eyes jokingly. "You know I love what we do here. It's not really work. And he's *not* Romeo. I made it very clear this is strictly professional."

Evelyn nodded and failed to hide a grin. "Sure, sure. Strictly professional people always buy ranches for their colleagues."

"He didn't buy it for *me*! It's a new project!" Evelyn just tipped her head and stared at me. For a moment, she almost reminded me of my mother. "Look, okay, we're friends, at best. Friend-*ly*. He's just…easy to be around." I sighed, refusing to admit I might actually be developing real feelings for Ben. "He reminds me of home, actually. The way so many Newfoundlanders are."

She grabbed her purse from the floor by the chair. "Is he from Newfoundland?"

I shook my head. "No, he's from somewhere down South, but I think his family was in the navy or something. He's got a ton of old nautical stuff and weapons."

"Like at your grandmother's?" She shivered with exaggeration.

I laughed, recalling the year I brought Evelyn home for Christmas. My Nan's sweet sword collection belonged in a museum, where most of her stuff already was. Evelyn, forever the sheltered city girl, loved the change of scenery but was unnerved by how many weapons my grandmother displayed around her house.

My heart squeezed as I realized…that was the last time I'd gone home.

***

Ben and I sat in the open space of his house boat home office, a place I'd come to love over the weeks, despite the onslaught of nightmares that hacked away at me at night. I lounged in a comfy leather chair, reviewing the budget for the ranch and approving progress reports for the resort as Ben rocked in his desk chair, a pair of dark-rimmed glasses inched to the tip of his nose.

I sat upright and rubbed my eyes. "I think I'm calling it a night."

"Dinner?" he suggested hopefully, setting his glasses on the desk.

"No, I really should get some sleep. I have to start the new plans for the ranch additions in the morning."

He grinned and rested his chin atop folded hands, eyelashes batting. "I'm sure it can wait a day; I hear the owner is pretty easy going."

I laughed, stuffing my things inside my bag. "Is that so?"

"Yup," he replied with that stupid smile I'd come to love. He stood from the chair and sauntered toward me. "But I actually have a question to ask you, and I'd prefer to do it over a good meal. There's a new seafood place downtown. Care to join me?"

A question? My heart stilled in my chest. I almost wanted to say no for fear of where it might lead. Was he going to ask me on a date? Was he going to ask me to take on even more work? Part of me worried about either possibility because I wasn't sure I had it in me to deny him. *Just politely decline*, I told myself. But one look at that hopeful, playful smile and the gleam in his soft brown eyes…

"I mean, as a Newfoundlander, am I even allowed to refuse the promise of seafood?" He opened his mouth to speak, and I quickly added, "As long as it's a work dinner."

"Of course," he replied coyly. "What else would it be?"

The new seafood place was a beautiful restaurant converted from an old warehouse with a cozy outdoor patio area for the warmer months. We opted for a table out there, half surrounded by trees, the other half open to the river. City lights sparkled off the water and danced with the soft lighting the restaurant had hung from wooden posts. Somewhere, a piano played melodies loud enough to warm my ears and allow for casual conversation.

"So, what are you in the mood for?" Ben asked as he scanned the single-page menu. He seemed nervous, although he hid it well. But being with him almost twenty-four-seven these last few weeks, I'd come to map out his usual body language.

I didn't comment on his fidgeting or bouncing leg; I just read over my own menu. "They have a sampler feast, a little bit over everything form the menu."

"Sounds perfect," he replied and smiled up at the waitress that appeared at our table. He ordered for us, and she took our menus as she left.

"So," I said, braiding my fingers together as I peered across the table at him. "What's this big important question?"

Ben took a massively deep breath and tucked his soft brown wave behind both ears. A pit began to form in my stomach. Either this was so bad he had to soften the blow with a nice meal, or it was so good he was worried about my reaction. Either way, the ball of nerves began to tangle in my gut.

His eyes locked on mine. "I would like you to be my partner."

My heart gave one big thwomp in my chest as I swallowed dryly. "What?"

"Business partner," he clarified. "I'm good with the hands-on stuff and sweat equity. Not so much with making things pretty and keeping things organized. Ace, I'd love to partner with you and give you a share in my company."

I didn't know what to say. The waitress brought our drinks, and I downed my whole glass of white wine. It didn't sit well in my stomach. "Ben…I…this is a huge proposal."

He managed a slightly shaky smile. "Well, it's not

marriage, but pretty darn close to it. You make every-thing I do better, Ace. We've been a team since day one, and everything we've done has turned into gold. You can't deny that this is a great idea."

I nodded, contemplating all the details. "You're not wrong. You've got the muscle, capital, and connections. I've got the brains and eye for design. On paper, this is a match made in heaven. But…"

"But what?" Those big brown eyes glistened, waiting for the answer he already knew.

But we have feelings for one another.

Our food arrived, saving me from having to say the words I'd been afraid of for weeks. I didn't *do* feelings; I didn't *do* relationships. But Benjamin Cook barrelled into my life and consumed every inch of it. I woke up eager to work with him each day, and I went to bed each night, anxious to start the next day.

Could I really become business partners with someone I thought of in that way? Could he keep himself in check and not constantly tease the fact that he was attracted to me? Part of me sometimes hoped he was just kidding, be-ing playful. But I knew it; I saw it in his eyes every time I looked at him.

I chewed at the inside of my cheek. "Could I still take other clients?"

"Of course." He let his lungs relax and smoothed his

hand over his beard as he slipped a finger through half a dozen calamari rings and popped one in his mouth. "It's your business and would remain so. I could take Ace Design on as our in-house designer on a non-exclusive basis. You'd still take whatever outside projects you can get." He popped two more rings in his mouth and shoved them to the side. "Not that you'd need to. I've got a lot of projects, Ace. You'd be set for life."

Just then, my phone pulsed on the table, startling me. I didn't even check the screen before pressing the side button and stuffing it in my pocket. I mulled over the grand proposal as I ate calamari and sipped from the little bowl of chowder in front of me.

I lobbed off a bite of garlic bread. "God, I don't know, Ben. This is huge."

"I know, I know." He nodded, continuing to stuff his face with seafood. "Take all the time you need to make a decision. But I thought we could discuss the details and lay everything out."

My phone vibrated against my side, but I ignored it. I plucked a steamed crab leg from a bowl and scooped the meat from the pre-cut slit. I didn't have the right words to give him any sort of response because all I could think of was my growing feelings for him. I didn't want it to get in the way of business and vice versa.

If I were being honest with myself, I think a part of me

had been waiting this whole time for our projects to wrap up, so we might take a chance and see where a relationship could lead outside of the bias of work.

My phone buzzed again, and I groaned with annoyance as I quickly checked the screen. It was my mother. I rolled my eyes and stuffed it in my purse.

"What's holding you back?" he asked. "How can I ease your mind?"

We stared at one another over the table. He knew the answer to that just as well as I did. But neither of us wanted to admit the deep, very real feelings budding between us.

I opened my mouth to speak but–even from my bag on the floor–the sound of my phone could be heard.

"Maybe you should get that," Ben suggested.

"It's just my mother." I waved it off.

"Well, your mother has called you three times in the last few minutes. Could be an emergency."

I chortled. "With my mom, everything's an emergency. She's probably calling to berate me for not coming home again this year."

Ben smiled, his eyes going distant. "You should be thankful you still have a mother on this earth who loves you enough to care."

I tipped my head as I stared at him. "Your mother's no longer here?"

"No, I'm afraid she died a long time ago." Sadness tinged his expression as he seemed to recall a memory. "I actually don't have any family left alive today."

"Oh, Ben, I'm so sorry." I reached across the table and took his warm hand in mine. "What happened to them?" He was about to answer when my phone vibrated again. I groaned. "I'm just going to turn it off."

"No, Ace, maybe you really should answer it. I wouldn't call anyone that many times if it weren't an emergency."

I huffed a sigh and fetched the device from my bag. "Fine." I pressed the green button and put the phone to my ear as I swiveled in my seat to face away from the table. "Mom?"

"Why haven't you been answering my calls?" Her voice came through the line with an emotional quiver. She sounded like she'd been crying.

"Mom, what's wrong?"

"Your grandmother…" She paused to pull herself together. "She died last night."

That nagging pit in the bottom of my stomach burned and sent my blood searing. I had to tell myself to breath. My nan was like another mother to me.

"Oh, God, Mom…"

"She's been sick for a few weeks," she said. "I'd been trying to reach you, but you never answer your god-forsaken phone. Too busy for your family, or what? Your brother calls me every night!"

"Mom! He's in his seven millionth year of university studying *mythology*. He has a bit more free time than I do." I tried to keep my voice low, but it was hard to hide my annoyance. She called to tell me my grandmother had died, but it only took half a second for her to scold me. I inhaled deeply through my nose. "I'm sorry. We shouldn't be fighting right now. How are you? How's dad? When's the funeral?"

"It's this Friday," she replied. Just two days from now. "Your brother's on his way home from Halifax. He's driving because there are no flights available until Monday."

"Okay, I'll see what I can get right now and be home as soon as possible." I swallowed nervously, the pit rising in my gut. "I love you, Mom."

"Love you, too." I could hear her failing to hold back tears. "See you soon."

She hung up, and I just stared at my blank phone screen momentarily, unable to focus on anything besides my searing veins and bloating stomach. Bile inched up my throat.

"Ace?" Ben said softly from my side. His shadow loomed over me, and he squatted to see my face. "Jesus, you okay?"

The words that rose were hardly my own. "M-my…nan passed away."

"Oh, Ace." His voice was soothing as he caressed my

cheek, and a tear ran down it. He just rubbed the droplet with his thumb. "I'm so sorry. I take it you were close?"

I just nodded as more tears spilled over. But that wasn't the only thing happening inside me. My unreliable stomach had reached its limit, and the contents surged upward. I scrambled out of my seat and dove for the trees just as every bit of seafood and wine shot out, ravaging my throat.

Ben was right there, holding my hair back and rubbing slow circles over my back. He asked the waitress to bring some water and fresh napkins, and she did it within seconds. I gagged on the remnants of vomit for a few moments before I sucked in a deep but shaky breath and let Ben ease me into a sitting position. I was thankful only two other tables were occupied, and the guests pretended not to notice the scene.

I wiped my face with the crisp white napkin.

"What can I do?" Ben asked. "What do you need?"

Thoughts were scrambled, and I fought to sift through them. "I…I need to book a flight home. Can you grab my phone?"

He only had to reach with one long arm to get it from the table. I checked for flights with trembling fingers, but nothing was available from Edmonton to Newfoundland until Sunday evening. I didn't have the option to just drive home like my brother did. Halifax was barely a day's drive, including the ferry. I'd have to drive across the country, and

I couldn't do that in a couple of days.

"Damn it!" A new onslaught of tears came, ones of frustration, and I slammed my phone down. "Stupid fucking tourist season!"

"What's wrong?" Ben asked.

"I can't leave here until Sunday; the funeral's this Friday."

He slipped a hand under my elbow and eased me to my feet. We stepped off to the side for more privacy, and I didn't say a thing as he wiped the tears from my face with a contemplative look.

"I have a plane," he said.

I guffawed and sniffled a bit of snot building in my nose. "Of course you do."

He chuckled lightly. "No, listen. It's small, but I can probably get us out of here by tomorrow."

"Us?"

His eyes widened. "Well, no, I didn't mean…I would have to accompany you on the flight to avoid extra red tape."

"Oh, I don't know, Ben, I couldn't ask–"

"You're not asking; I'm offering." When I didn't answer, he added, "Look, I can use the time to scope out a few properties if that'll make you feel better about it. Consider it a work trip. You're just hitching a ride."

The hope in his eyes, the sound of his voice, and just the simple nearness of him calmed my nerves, and I found myself able to take a slow, deep breath and make sense of my thoughts. It was my only shot to get home in time for Nan's funeral, and I simply couldn't miss it.

So, I gave him a quick nod before I changed my mind. "Okay, if you can, I'll take the offer."

Ben lit up, clearly ecstatic that he could help in any way. "I'll call and arrange it right now."

He turned and got on the phone with someone while I walked back to the table to gather my stuff, unable to truly believe she was gone. I'd avoided going home for years and kept telling myself I had time.

But I knew better than most…time was a son of a bitch.

CHAPTER FOUR

BEN

If Ace ever found out how much I paid to arrange this flight, she'd kill me on the spot. I was sure of it. So, I sat across from her and watched her stare out the window, content with being near her. If these last few months had taught me anything, it was that no matter how old you are, someone can always come along and make you feel like your life had always been on autopilot.

Even if you're hundreds of years old.

I brushed the thought away, just as I had several times since meeting Ace. At first, I tried to convince myself she was just another pretty face. But, with every passing second I spent in her presence, it became impossible to deny that something in me reached for her.

I hadn't felt like that in a very long time, and it was getting harder to stop myself from pursuing something more with her. My heart had always been a wild creature, but my rational mind kept conjuring one image that kept me in my place; Ace, aging beautifully, dying in a bed surrounded by silver curls, and me…exactly as I am today. Never aging, never dying.

Immortality. It was a gift and a curse, but one I'd endure over and over again if it meant saving the woman who'd given me everything so many years ago. I sometimes thought of Dianna, wondered where she was and what life she lived after I traded my soul for hers. I knew I could have tracked her down and paid her a visit, especially now that my immortal existence had finally caught up with her.

But I'd made a promise to myself that day on the beach. As she walked away from me, I swore to never look back. And I hadn't. I never tried to find her because that wasn't our story; that wasn't our end. Dianna was a connection like nothing else. She was my friend, my sister, and my other half. We shared a soul, in a way. Fate had bound us together to save one another.

And we did.

Our story ended that day, and I'd spent the last three hundred years trying to find where mine was supposed to lead. I'd almost given up hope until I saw Ace that day with her measuring tape, the sun gleaming off her diamond-white curls. I immediately knew I had to do whatever it took to have her in my life. But part of me was grateful she insisted on keeping things professional between us because that image of a beautiful, dying woman with her wrinkled hand in mine… It was unfair to her.

As much as my heart may want her, I could never doom her to that life. So, I'd settle for this, for what we had.

"You might want to consider blinking," I teased, the first words either of us had spoken since we took off a couple of hours ago.

She slowly peeled her gaze from the window and stared at me with a level of sadness that made my heart ache. Sadness and something else. What was going on behind those enchanting eyes?

"You okay, Ace? You want something to eat?" she shook her head. "Drink?" Another head shake. She returned to staring blankly out the little window.

I sighed and grabbed a sub sandwich and two bottles of water from the mini-fridge. I set them on the little round table between us and cut the sub into several pieces before stuffing one in my mouth.

"Mmm, damn, I love these sandwiches," I said, chewing with one side of my mouth. "They put the perfect amount of mayonnaise to mustard ratio." I swallowed the food and cracked the top on one of the waters. I took a long swig and let out an exaggerated sound of satisfaction. "Refreshing."

Without a word, Ace picked one of the sandwich pieces off the plate and started nibbling on it. I couldn't ignore the little sigh of relief that turned over in my chest. She hadn't eaten all day, and I worried she wouldn't eat at all. Was it just the grief of losing her grandmother that plagued her? Or did something else chip away at that beautiful heart of hers? I didn't dare ask.

The rest of the trip went much like that, me casually sticking food and beverages in front of her, hoping she'd put sustenance in her body. Pretending to sleep so she'd feel comfortable enough to nap. When we landed, she finally spoke.

"I'll see if I can get us a couple rental cars."

I nodded. "I'll get our bags and meet you out front."

I watched through the window as she made her way across the Tarmac. She carried a weight on her shoulders I'd never seen before. Gone was the fun, carefree business partner and friend. Coming home to Newfoundland was doing something to Ace, eating her up inside, and it killed me to watch it.

I found her waiting outside the car rental office, arms crossed and cheeks red with anger. I set the bags down on the sidewalk.

"You okay?"

"There's only one rental vehicle available," she huffed. "I fucking *hate* tourist season!" She turned and kicked the brick wall.

"Hey, hey, it's okay." I placed a gentle hand on her arm. "Ace, It's fine. I'll just drive you to your parent's house then I'll take the car from there and find a hotel somewhere. I'll pick you up in a few days, and we'll go home. Easy." She paced in place, stewing. "How far is your parent's place from here?"

"About an hour."

I shrugged it off. "Awesome! Let's go, then. I'll drive, you direct."

She lifted her heavy gaze and looked into my eyes. "You'll never get a hotel room this time of year. Everything's been pre-booked for months. Just stay with us; we have plenty of room."

I chuckled, rubbing the back of my neck nervously. "Ace, this isn't a warm family visit. You're here for your grandmother's funeral."

I witnessed a slight upward tug at the corner of her mouth, and my heart skipped a beat. I'd give anything to see her smile right now. "Trust me, my mother wouldn't have it any other way. The man who got her daughter home against all odds? It's the Newfoundland way; we treat strangers like family." She gave me two hard pats on my arm and began walking toward the car. "They even made a musical about it.”

We loaded up the little hybrid SUV, left the airport, and headed toward the highway. Ace’s directions were simple; follow the highway straight to the Rocky Harbour off-ramp. Newfoundland was so much untouched, raw beauty. Summer was in full swing, and the thick trees lined both sides of the Trans Canada.

Aside from a gas station and a Tim Horton’s, there wasn’t much of anything besides a gorgeous landscape worthy of a postcard or some fancy coffee table book. It reminded me of just how far man had come in three hundred years and that I’d been hunkered down in big cities for far too long. I missed the sea.

Ace was silent and stared out the window. I caught the passing greenery flickering over her unblinking eyes, now rimmed with soft, reddish-purple skin.

“Hey, I know I sound like a broken record over here,” I said, breaking her from the weird trance that seemed to hold her. “But I’m worried about you, Ace. And, at the risk of you biting my head off for sticking my nose in your business, is something else bothering you? This doesn’t feel like run-of-the-mill grieving.”

She tried to sigh, but the air fettered in her chest, and she pressed her lips together to stop herself from tearing up. “I left this island the day I graduated high school. I didn’t even go to my own graduation ceremony. I just…

needed to get away. Needed to…leave it all behind."

I swallowed dryly. "Bad childhood?"

"No, not like that," she replied. "My parents are amazing, wonderful people." She pointed to a turn-off. "Take this exit."

We veered off the busy–busy for rural Newfoundland–highway and made our way into the quaint seas-side town of Rocky Harbour. Backyard clotheslines hung low with fresh white sheets, kids ran and played together, and tourists walked about, pointing and admiring all the small-town attractions.

"Keep driving down this main drag," she instructed. "Until you come to a three-way stop. Then take a right."

I did as she said. "So, this is where you grew up?"

Ace sucked in a long, deep breath threw her nose. "Yeah, this is home." She pointed at a building. "That's my family's bakery; my mom and nan ran it together. I guess it's just my mom now."

I threw her a sideways grin. "No desire to take over the family business?"

She laughed, and the sound coddled my heart. "God, no. I didn't inherit the Cobham women's ability in the kitchen."

Stone-cold panic punched me in the chest, and I almost lost control of the car. "What did you say?" I asked, my voice cracking as I steadied the vehicle on the road, which turned from pavement to groomed gravel.

Ace went wide-eyed, hands braced against the door and dashboard. "I-I mean, I can follow a recipe if I have a gun to my head, but–"

"No, no. The *name*." My throat tightened. "Did you say *Cobham*?"

An old cape cod blue house appeared in the distance, cutting the sky, and my brain refused to connect the sight of it with the images I'd once conjured up from stories I was told.

"Yeah, it's my mother's name."

My breathing quickened, and my head spun as the steering wheel slipped under my moist palms. "Ace," I whispered, struggling to work through my racing thoughts. "Ace *White*." I eased off the gas as we approached the house at the end of the lane. An older but familiar-looking man with blonde hair leaned on the front deck railing with a drink in hand. His familiar coal-black eyes peered curiously at the car.

"Ben?" she said. "What's wrong? You're freaking me out."

I turned and looked at her, seeing her in a completely different light. Curls like her mother's but the color of her father's hair. The roundness of her face, the dark pits that stared back at me. "Audrey?"

Her eyes widened. "How did you–"

"You're Audrey Cobham?"

"Well, Audrey White, actually."

Of course. I dragged my gaze back to the man on the deck just as a beautiful older woman stepped to his side. Her long black curls were pinned back loosely, revealing streaks of silver underneath. She narrowed her eyes, trying to tell who was in the car, and she smiled when Ace waved. But when those soft brown eyes flitted to me in the driver's seat, her face paled, and she grabbed her husband's arm with one hand while the other covered her mouth.

"Ben, what's going on?" She glanced back and forth between her parents and me. "Do you know my mom and dad or something?"

A sound of disbelief burped from me, and I ran both hands through my hair as I stared unblinkingly at two people I thought I'd never see again. "You could say that." I opened the door, stepped out of the car, and gripped the edge of it for dear life as Ace's mother came down the few steps to the driveway. I managed a shaky smile as tears formed in her eyes. "Hello, Dianna."

She took one quick breath and fainted.

***

I sat on the back porch and watched Ben in the distance, the sun setting on the horizon over the water, as he kicked around the sand on the beach by our house and muttered things to himself in anger. The patio door slid open behind me, and Dad sat down and handed me a steaming cup of tea.

"Is Mom okay?"

He stared at Ben on the beach with an unreadable look. "She'll be fine." He sipped his tea the same way I always did—sometimes, looking at my father was like looking at an older, alternate version of myself. "How did you get mixed up with him?"

The way Dad spoke of Ben…I couldn't tell if he liked him or not. "He's a client."

He tore his gaze away and stared at me, so many emotions burning in his eyes. "Did he seek you out? Did he know who you were?"

I shook my head. "No, he figured it out as we pulled into the driveway. He assumed my real name was Ace the whole time."

The corner of Dad's mouth turned up. He'd given me the nickname Ace when I was ten. School had always been a breeze. I never studied, yet somehow always brought home straight As. "Well, you haven't gone by Audrey in years."

I took a cleansing breath and set my tea down on the step beside me. "I just had to start fresh, you know?" He nodded. Dad always understood me in a way no one else could. "I never want to forget my life here, but I had to leave it behind, in a sense."

"And the nightmares?"

I tried my best to keep it cool, but I couldn't lie to my father, even if I wanted to. The patio door slid open again, and my mother stepped out, saving me from having to divulge that the dreams still plagued me despite the distance I put between myself and the ocean. But Dad eyed me curiously over his mug, and when our gazes crossed, I knew he knew. Sadness and worry stared back at me.

I peered up at Mom and forced a tired smile. "Are you alright?"

"Yes," she replied, her attention on the beach as she clutched her wool sweater closed with both hands. I'd never seen my mother so pale. "Just…it's a lot." She took a seat between Dad and me on the wide step. "With Mom's passing, being so busy at the bakery, and now this–" She gestured at Ben in the distance and shook her head.

I placed a hand on her back. "I'm sorry, Mom. For not calling more or making time to come home and visit." I chewed at my lip. "And, I guess, for bringing Ben here. But I had no idea… I-I still don't understand."

"And how could you?" Dad said. "You had no knowledge of him."

I rubbed my fingertips over my dry lips, every nerve inside me scattered. "Uncle Finn, Gus, and Aunt Lottie.

Even little Charlie. All the stuff about Maria Cobham and the crazy adventure you guys had…." A pit festered in my gut. "You never once mentioned anyone named Ben. Why?"

My parents exchanged a look, and my dad kissed her cheek before standing up. "I'll give you some space, love." And he slowly made his way down the hill behind out house that led to the beach.

Mom just stared unblinking at the two men, but she wasn't *looking* at them but rather…past them to another place, another time. "I remember when you were first taken." Her voice quivered. "The four of us were happy, laying on the beach, a picnic spread out around us as you and Arthur played by the water. One second, you were there, laughing. The next minute Arthur said you were gone."

"But you and Dad found me within minutes."

She closed her eyes tightly, squeezing out the tears that had formed. They ran down her soft cheeks, and she quickly wiped them away before I could reach out. "I should have seen it for what it was, a threat. She took you both not long after."

I swallowed dryly, my throat threatening to close off at the memory I'd buried so deeply. The siren and all her nightmarish glory. The thing that haunted my dreams. The half-insane creature of the sea kidnapped my twin brother and me and took us not only to another place but another time. All because of some stupid Cobham curse.

"What does Ben have to do with all of it?"

"He's like your father," she replied. "He's from the past."

"What?" A coldness took hold of my chest. The old trinkets, the vintage maps, and the love of old properties. Of course, it made so much sense now. He wasn't a collector…those were things from his life. "But how did he get here? Did he come with you guys?"

Mom tipped her head to the darkening sky and breathed deeply before fetching a small stack of leather-bound journals from inside her chunky sweater. One thin and black, another a deep red, and one thick brown journal loaded with extra papers and corners of images sticking out. All three were held together with a few wraps of twine.

"It's all in here," she said and handed the books to me. "It'll all make sense when you read these. The red was your grandmother's, the black was your father's from when he was a boy, and the brown journal…." She gave it an endearing smile. "It's mine. Everything you need to know is contained within these books; our adventure, our loss, our story–" Mom cupped my cool cheek in her warm hand. "And yours."

CHAPTER FIVE

BEN

The footsteps that approached were too heavy to be female. I knew exactly who was headed toward the beach I paced on, and I waited for him with my back turned, not ready for the inevitable conversation. Not ready for any of this.

I'd made a promise to myself years ago that I'd let them be, that I wouldn't let my immortal existence touch theirs, that I'd wait until they had lived a lifetime and then I could finally let out the breath I'd been holding in for three hundred years. It was the least I could do after what I'd done, the foolish wish I'd made that night on the beach beside The Siren's Call. Even giving up my soul wasn't enough.

Nothing would ever be enough.

Did Audrey know? Was she aware of who I *really* was? The mistakes I'd made, the trouble I'd caused. A single wish had taken us all down a tragic road of twisted fates and death and led us all to ends that weren't filled happily ever afters.

Lottie had become a shell of a person in the years that followed, Finn had reluctantly returned to his home and accepted his birthright as Lord of the Artair Keep, and I had wandered the earth for hundreds of years.

I'd tried to find a purpose and discover love the way my heart desperately wanted. I quickly realized I'd never have that with Freya; her heart belonged to her home and people. And I was nothing but a plaything to Roselyn Wallace.

I gave up the hunt for that reciprocated kind of love a long time ago and searched for things that brought me joy instead. With no soul, I had eternity to figure out who I was. I could only hope that my sacrifice had given Dianna and Henry a fighting chance at happiness.

Henry came to a stop in the sand beside me. I didn't bother turning to look at him. We just stood there in silence for a few minutes, letting the sound of the gentle waves move through the air. Finally, he spoke.

"You know, I never got to thank you for what you did that day. For giving up your soul for Dianna."

I stuffed my hands in my pockets and toed the sand

with my boot. "It was the least I could have done."

"Because you loved her?"

The pain and curiosity in his voice made me look up, and I saw it…the look in his eyes that asked a question he must have held onto all these years. Was I still in love with his wife?

I tipped my head. "Yes and no. I think…" I wanted to be very clear and took a second to organize my thoughts. "I think, over a hundred years on a cursed ship being forced to feed my brother's cannibalistic crew…I would have fallen in love with the first person who came along and showed me a morsel of humanity. Dianna risked everything to save me, and I was filled with gratitude. I admired her, and I felt indebted to her. She gave me a second chance, and I woke up every day worried I'd never be able to make it up to her."

Henry nodded, his expression pensive. I didn't really answer his question.

"I'm not in love with your wife, Henry," I assured him. "I don't think I ever was. Not like that."

His shoulders softened, and he let out a long breath. "And what about my daughter?"

"Look, man, I just want you to know that this is just as weird for me as it is for you," I told him honestly. "I never planned this. I had no idea who she was, and if I had…."

"Would it have changed anything?"

I thought for a moment. I was pretty sure I'd fallen in love with Ace the moment I laid eyes on her. Within seconds of speaking with her, I knew, deep down, I would do whatever it took to be in her life.

I hung my head. "I'm not sure."

Henry patted me on the back with a tired chuckle. "Relax. Audrey's never gotten serious with anyone; she won't let them get close enough. If it's you...." He gave it a moment of thought but then smiled. "I'd be glad."

I guffawed. "I thought you hated my guts."

"I did," Henry replied without hesitation. "At first. But I grew to respect and appreciate your role in Dianna's life—in all our lives. Eventually, I realized any hatred I had toward you was really jealousy because I always knew you were good enough for her, for Dianna. And it killed me knowing that she could have chosen you at any moment."

"But she chose you, time and time again," I said. "It's always been you, man."

"I thank my lucky stars every God damn day."

I clapped him on the shoulder, a new and mutual understanding now concrete between us. "You better."

CHAPTER

SIX

AUDREY

Every step toward the ocean raked at my nerves, but I had to go talk to Ben. I had no idea what he and my father spoke about, but as Dad turned and headed back to the house, he looked peaceful. We met halfway down the hill that led to the beach, and he stopped to give me a smile.

We exchanged no words, just a look of understanding. He gave me a nod and a kiss on my forehead before walking back to the house behind me. I cradled the journals close to my chest and stopped where the grass turned to sand, refusing to get any closer to the water. The ocean screamed in my head, and I gritted my teeth to black it out.

"Ben?"

He spun around, face alight with a look of hope. He eyed me up and down, noting my feet firmly planted, and walked toward me.

"So, can you really not swim, or is that just what you tell people?"

My lip trembled as I stared over his shoulder at the living nightmare. "No, after we returned," I swallowed tightly—I couldn't believe I was talking about this with someone other than my family. "After everything...I never learned to swim."

He considered it and rocked back on his heels with his hands in his pockets. "I get it."

"So, can you live forever or something?"

Ben looked at me with a saddened smile. "Or something." His attention fell to the books in my hands, and he motioned to them. "It's all written in those pages, I bet."

Everything in me wanted to bolt, to put as much distance between myself and that ocean as possible. "How fucking old *are* you?"

Ben tilted his head, a calculating look of regret on his handsome face. "I don't know if you'll like that answer."

I let out a puff of air. "Please, my dad is hundreds of years old. I can handle it." I quickly wiped away a bit of wetness around my eyes. "And I think I have a right to know. Nothing happened between us, but something's there, right? I'm not crazy? You…have feelings for me?"

He slowly nodded, and I could see the hesitation, laced with guilt. What plagued him so badly?

"I was born sometime in the late fifteen hundreds and spent over a hundred years on a cursed pirate ship when your mother found me and broke the curse."

Part of me had a feeling those were just the footnotes. I knew there was far more to the story than that. There had to be. Mom said I'd find it all in the journals.

My breathing quickened, approaching panic, and I knew I had to go. The sea was just too much for me, especially having been removed from it for so long. I'd almost forgotten the hold it had over me.

I took one step back. "I'm, uh, I'm going to stay at my nan's just down the road." I waggled the stack of leather books.

Ben nodded in understanding. "Of course."

I wanted to run to him, hug him and find that feeling that had taken residence within me these last few weeks. Safety, warmth, and everything Ben's presence made me feel. But I had to sort out this story first to figure out where his piece fit in the grand and tragic adventure of my parents' lives.

And mine.

"If you want to talk, that's where you'll find me." I started walking away, relieved to be putting distance between myself and the sea, but an ache formed in my heart to leave him there.

"Ace?" he called softly. I glanced over my shoulder and almost wept at the pain in his eyes. "I'm sorry."

My brows pinched together. "For what?"

His gaze dropped to the books tucked under my arm. "You'll see."

***

Nan's old house—once my great aunt's—was just a short walk to the other end of the gravel lane my family lived on. I turned the old brass knob and took a moment to inhale the scent of my childhood. Baked goods, fresh line-dried linens, and remnants of a burning wood stove.

After we returned from the past, it didn't take long for me to feel suffocated by my worried, paranoid mother. Art, my brother, lapped it up like the little mama's boy he still is today.

My grandmother's house was the only place Mom let me go without worrying, so I practically lived there. When I was a teenager, Nan converted her only spare bedroom into one just for me. The reading of the will wasn't until Saturday, but I already knew this house was mine. Nan had told me a million times, and everyone knew it.

The little saltbox house was filled with a summer

evening chill, so I lit the woodstove and raided Nan's liquor cabinet. I claimed a half-finished bottle of screech and stood in the kitchen, staring at the stack of journals on the table.

Part of me was scared to read them, fearing what I'd find. What if I discovered my life was a lie? What if I found out something horrible about my parents? But Mom and Ben seemed to think I'd find all the answers I needed in those pages. I took one long swig of rum and pulled the red one off the top while the golden liquor warmed my belly.

And I read.

I had no idea how much time had passed as I sat and leaned against every surface of my grandmother's kitchen, but I read every page of those three journals and polished off the bottle. I found no lies, deceit, or anything damning about the people I loved. The story was the same one I grew up with; the journals just filled in some holes.

It all began with Constance, my grandmother. She was born in the sixteen hundreds and was raised by a coven of Gaelic witches called The Keepers of Time. Nan had messed with things and tumbled through time only to end up here in the future just before my mother was born. Nan met a man named Arthur Sheppard and fell in love. She stayed here, married him, and gave birth to my mother. The Keepers were furious, though. She didn't belong here, and they eventually found a way to drag her back to her own time.

Nan mourned the loss of her husband and child, so she went to the sirens and wished for a child to fill the hole in her heart. But the beasts never give willingly and never without a price. They agreed to give her a baby in exchange for completing an impossible task: get back the stolen siren's heart from the men who stole it.

I knew the story; I had always known the details except for the fact that one of those men was Benjamin Cook, and the task was impossible because the crew was stuck aboard a cursed ship tethered to an island that didn't exist.

Of course, my grandmother failed the task, despite trying. So, the sirens gave her a cursed child, a half-siren, and a mentally insane daughter named Maria Cobham. Maria grew up to become one of the most ruthless pirates to ever sail the seas and kidnapped a young man to do her bidding. That man would eventually become my father, Captain Devil-Eyed Barrett.

Here in the present, my mother was living her life in Edmonton when Grandpa Arthur died. She flew home for the funeral and accidentally broke an enchanted ship-in-a-bottle which sent her back in time to the seventeen hundreds, where she was taken prisoner aboard a pirate ship captained by my father. But she quickly weaseled her way in with them by becoming the ship's cook, and Dad fell in love with her.

They came here to the future, had my brother and me, and built a nice, quiet, safe life for themselves. But a deranged siren kidnapped Arthur and me when we were four, took us back in time, and my parents came after us. With the help of their old crew, they saved us and returned home.

That's where they story always stopped for me. It was why I feared the sea. I never really drowned. That's just what I told people. But turns out I didn't have all the details, either.

Cut to the middle of the story, when my parents stopped Maria and saved my grandmother. They didn't just sail North and save her. No, the story wasn't as simple as that, and the journals painted a whole new picture for me.

While sailing to England, their ship hit a bad storm, and my mom was separated from them. She washed up on a deserted island with no hope of being saved. But that same island was the one Ben's cursed ship was tethered to, the one that held the siren's heart my grandmother failed to find.

My mom saved them all, returned the siren's heart, and the sea beasts gave her three wish pearls as a reward. That's how they found Maria and saved my grandmother, and returned home to the future.

But the sirens weren't done. Their eternal grudge against

the Cobham women was unwarranted and ridiculous, but it didn't stop them from meddling in our lives. While my parents were happy here in the future raising Arthur and me, Ben was in the past mourning the loss of the woman who had saved him, and a rogue siren took advantage of his pain. She tricked him into wishing to see my mother again, which led the creature to kidnap my brother and me to lure Mom back to the past.

I stacked the books on the table again and wandered to the wide back patio looking out over the ocean. The moon was a giant silver coin in the sky and glittered over the water's surface. It was a calm night, but the sea still screamed in my head. Angry that I wouldn't listen, annoyed that I refused to step foot inside it.

As a kid, it would call me at night, and I would sleep walk down to the beach, where my grandmother or parents would find me shortly after. The sleepwalking continued even after we returned from the past. But I didn't remember what happened while I paced the wet sands. Every instance was a dark spot in my mind. I picked at the chipping paint on the patio step as a thought occurred to me.

Ben must feel guilty for everything that happened; that's what he must have meant when he apologized earlier. But the taunting and the sleepwalking began before the siren ever kidnapped us. Long before Ben had made that stupid wish.

Maybe it wasn't his fault after all.

With a huff, I pushed to my feet and headed back inside, where I wandered about Nan's house. I missed her dearly, and being there, amongst all the things that made her life, hurt my heart. She'd practically raised me, and I couldn't even find the time to call her more than a handful of times since I'd left home.

I swiped another bottle from the cabinet, some other kind of rum she loved, and drank long swigs while I walked through the house. My room was exactly as I'd left it; a handmade quilt over the little twin bed, a rickety old desk still covered in papers and books, and posters of Spike from Buffy. I swear, I could even smell faint whiffs of cotton candy perfume.

I laughed to myself and entered Nan's bedroom without thinking. For a split second, she lay on the bed, covered in her favorite wool blanket. A gasp turned cold in my throat, and I shook my head as I blinked away the mirage.

The room was dark and empty as I slowly lay where she always did, with a perfect view of the sea. I wanted to curl up and cry, to hold her pillow tight until I fell asleep and absorbed whatever scent of her was left. I rolled out the wool Afghan, and a piece of paper fell to the floor. It stared up at me with one word written in a familiar scrawl across the front.

Audrey.

I plucked it from the floor and opened the letter written in my Nan's handwriting.

Sweet girl, I know you're hurting right now, but rest assured, I'm in a better place. I'd lived a life only others could dream of, and every minute of it was filled with adventure, hope, and love. Love that you all blessed me with.

I know my time is nearing, so I am writing you this letter. There's an old trunk at the foot of my bed. Open it.

I wiped the tears and set the letter on the bed. The trunk was one I remembered well, every gorgeous detail right down to the rusted hinges. But I'd never seen it open. The lock hung loosely, so I removed it and lifted the creaky lid to reveal a collection of neatly packed items.

I unfolded two trench coats; a thick red one with big gold buttons and a black jacket made of soft, worn leather. I slipped my arms inside the leather one, and the long sleeve hung heavily. I rolled them up and continued searching through the treasures. Wooden trinket boxes, old pistols, and velvet satchels held closed with thick drawstrings. I found a fortune in mixed gems and rough-cut coins when I pulled one open. There were three other bags like that.

"What the hell?" I whispered to myself and grabbed Nan's note again.

When your mother found her way back that final time, she made me swear to get rid of everything, every tie to the past. She wanted to start fresh and give you the best possible chance of a normal life. You see, sweet girl, items from the past have tethers and, with the right magic, can pull us back just as they can pull us forward.

But I watched you for years, having nightmares and walking dreams. I fetched you from the water more times than I can count, just as your parents often did. I knew it wasn't mere nightmares, though. You were being called.

The sirens aren't done with the Cobham women, and we had to protect you, whatever it took. It's why your mother urged you to pursue a life far from the water.

But, my angel, you're not a child anymore, but I suspect those nightmares still plague you. I tried all your life to figure out what the sirens wanted with you or who might be calling you from the past. I kept track of every instance, every nightmare, and every clue I found. It's all documented in the journal.

I looked up from the paper and searched the trunk. Sure enough, there was a navy-blue leather-bound journal.

Take it, and look at the pieces. Perhaps you can see how to put together the puzzle and figure out what they want. Put an end to it and break this generational curse. But, never make a deal with a siren, and don't make the same mistakes I did.

I love you, sweet girl.

P.S. You know the house is yours. Give your brother a share of the treasure found in the trunk.

Nan

I opened the journal, my head swimming from the rum, and skimmed my grandmother's notes. Dates and times, descriptions, drawings, and Polaroids of each time she pulled me away from the beach.

My heart thrummed in my ears as I stared at each image of the ghostly little girl. Soaked pajamas, eyes that should have been black like my father's were clouded over with a silvery gaze, and then some pictures even showed the ends of my hair crimped from being dipped in the water.

I didn't remember any of this.

I knew I'd had a problem with sleep walking as a kid, but not to this extent. I scanned the dates written in Nan's handwriting and did the math. The instances were scattered; sometimes, once a week, a couple times a month, but sometimes every night. How much had she told my parents? Why didn't anyone tell me how bad it really was?

"Ace?"

Ben's deep, raspy voice echoed through the empty halls of the house. I ran to the stairs but stopped as my body reminded me I was half-drunk, and I gripped the railing as I took each step carefully. He waited in the porch, and my heart sprang to life at the sight of him.

The muggy Newfoundland weather had his thin white t-shirt hugging every curve and line of his muscular body, and those soft brown waves I loved so much were pulled back into a messy knot. Maybe it was the rum, or maybe I'd finally grown tired of lying to myself, but I wanted to rake my hands over him, pull his hair from the tie, and put my mouth to his.

I crossed my arms tightly. "Hey."

He arched a brow. "Hey?"

"Welcome to my new house?" I added with a sarcastic sweep of my arm. "I dunno, Ben. What do you want me to say?" I gripped the edge of the table to steady myself.

"Are you drunk?"

"Only a lot."

He deflated but then stiffened again. "*What* are you wearing?"

"My new jacket. You like?" I did a clumsy spin.

"I can see this is a bad time to talk." He turned for the door. "I'll leave you be."

"No!" The word jumped from my mouth before I could think about it, and I grit my teeth. *Stupid.* "Don't go," I cringed and gave in to a heavy sigh. "Please." Ben stood in the porch, seemingly unsure if he could enter further. I gestured to the chairs. "Come in, have a seat."

He took a few careful steps toward me but didn't sit.

"Want a drink?" I offered.

He shook his head. "Did you…"

"Read the journals?" I finished for him, and he pursed his lips. "Yeah, I read them." His glistening eyes searched mine, trying to read me. "And I don't see any reason for you to be sorry."

"What?"

I managed a shaky smile as I closed the short distance between us and took his hand. Only then did I realize how clammy mine were. "Come with me."

The bottom of my jacket dragged over the hardwood as I led him upstairs to my Nan's bedroom, where I had the journals and things from the trunk spread out on the floor. Ben stared at it like I'd just brought him to a crime scene.

"I know you feel horrible for your wish and what it led to," I told him. "But the story doesn't add up. Not for me."

"What do you mean?" His voice cracked. "Ace, it nearly got you and your brother *killed*."

"Yes and no." I plucked all the Polaroids from the floor and fanned them out for him, and one look made him wince and look away. "My grandmother took these when I used to sleep walk. She thought the sea and the sirens were calling me."

"After you guys came back?"

I nodded. "But also, before we ever left. *Before* you made that wish." His face went ghostly white, and I let myself reach out and touch him to brush his scruffy cheek. But he barely noticed my hand. His expression was distant and reeling even as I swiped a stray tear with my thumb. "You were not the reason, Ben. You were the excuse the siren used to put her fucked up plans in motion."

He stepped away from my touch. "H-how can you be so sure?"

Three hundred years of guilt was going to be hard to wipe clean. I set the pictures down on the dresser. "My memories of it all are muddled, even completely blank in places. But Nan documented everything. I have all the pieces of the puzzle and all the proof I need to know that it wasn't your fault." I grabbed Nan's journal and began flipping through the entries, setting sparks to my buried memories. "You were a pawn, just like the rest of us."

Ben backed up, a blank look on his face, and sat on the bed. The old mattress bowed and sank under his massive weight, and I slunk to the floor at his feet as I made my way through the pages, scanning for dates and keywords. I leaned against his steady leg as blurry images formed in my mind, shaping Nan's words.

"This one is just weeks after we returned from the past," I said and read the entry out loud.

I fetched Audrey from the water for the third time this week. I stayed awake and waited until she crawled out of bed like a zombie and walked through the house with eerie silver eyes. I carefully followed close behind as she tottered to the beach and sank her toes in the sand. It took everything in me not to grab her and run back to the house, but I had to see. I had to know what the sirens wanted with my granddaughter because she could never remember.

But the creature knew I hid in the bushes and turned its devilish, otherworldly stare on me as it spoke just one sentence before it disappeared.

The Cobhams will pay, and she will be ours.

A shiver furled through me, and I tipped my head upward as Ben's massive hand rubbed circles over my back. "See? It was never about you. They have some grudge against Cobham women. I'm pretty sure the siren would have eventually taken me with or without your wish."

Ben rested his other elbow on his knee and leaned forward, pinching and rubbing the bridge of his nose. I wrapped my hand around his thick thigh, our faces dangerously close. I could feel his warm breath tickling my skin, inviting me closer. I wanted to wipe away the pain and regret in his eyes, to assure him that none of what happened was his fault and that he carried the burden for far too long.

I shifted to my knees and ran my fingers through his silky brown waves, our noses touching. But Ben placed his hand over mine with a new kind of worry in his eyes.

"Ace," he whispered. "What are you doing?"

"Something that I've wanted to do for a long time." I brushed my lips over his, testing his resolve.

"We shouldn't–"

"Give me one good reason why not." My mouth moved against his, and I felt his hand turn into a fist at my back. "I know you want me just as badly as I want you. Why are we fighting this?"

"I…I can't give you…." He had to pause to swallow

through the emotion bubbling up. "I'm immortal, Ace. I'll live forever while you grow old and *die*." The last word came out in a strained rasp.

I stood and crawled over his lap. "I'm not asking for forever. I just want right now." I held his head between both hands as I straddled him on the edge of the bed, forcing him to look at me. "Ben. Tell me I'm wrong. Tell me you don't want me, and I'll step away right now."

We both moved with the massive sigh that rolled through him, and I held his glazy stare as I molded my body to his, my heart beating wildly in my chest. I'd never been rejected in my life. Everything I ever wanted had always lined up in front of me like willing prey; school, friends, work, and men. Especially men.

Ben's hands splayed across my back beneath the jacket, holding me closer, and I tightened my legs around his waist. His nose caressed mine as he swayed his mouth back and forth in front of mine, taunting me. But I could sense the hesitation in him.

"Don't you want me, Benjamin Cook?" I teased and felt him growing beneath me.

"You have no idea." His fingers gently dug into my back and slowly moved to cup my ass, pulling me even closer.

I gave my hips a little roll, dragging over his pants. A low growl turned over from somewhere deep inside him, vibrating through me.

"What are you doing to me, Ace?"

I braided my fingers at the back of his head and grinned at his mouth. "I think that's pretty evident."

Mouths gaped, and hot breaths entwined as our warm bodies melded together; I took the first leap and kissed him. He stilled, chest heaving while those eternal eyes searched mine as if he expected me to change my mind. So, I kissed him again and again, relishing in those soft and plump lips, tasting the sweetness of his breath.

Something clicked, and Ben let go of whatever reservations held him back. I reached down and caressed the rock-hard bulge in his pants, and an audible shiver raked through him with a groan of desire. His mouth devoured mine with every kiss, refusing to break our bodies' only connection.

He ripped the buttons from my shirt with one swift yank, leaving it hanging open. I grappled for the hem of his t-shirt, and it disappeared in half a second. A little moan purred in my chest as more hot skin met his.

As soon as I touched the belt on his pants, Ben picked me up and flipped me onto the bed, my shirt and jacket flayed open to him. I watched impatiently as he stepped out of his pants and helped him haul mine off.

"May as well take the panties while you're standing," I told him with a devilish grin.

He stood there, half naked, his body heaving, and I

could tell he let doubt creep back in. "Ace, I don't know—"

"Ben?" I said sternly, and he raised his brows. "If you don't fuck my brains out right now, you can get back on that plane and go home."

His shoulders slumped helplessly, and my breath hitched at the sight of his giant muscles contracting beneath his lovely, tanned skin. He peered at me from beneath a darkened gaze, shadowed by his lowered brow that suddenly arched to one side.

"Yes, ma'am."

His body covered mine with flesh and heat that seared my skin, and two fingers gently massaged the folds between my legs, readying me. His lips crushed mine, and I welcomed it, dragging my teeth over his as he pulled away for air. I rolled my hips in an invitation, and Ben hooked one arm under my leg as he hoisted it over his shoulder and slowly slid inside me.

I gasped as I felt my body expanding, adapting to his sheer size, and he gently eased further and further. My fingers dug into his soft skin, feeling his back muscles contracting with every careful movement. I grabbed his head and kissed him hard just as he plunged himself to the hilt, and I cried out with the pain of pleasure.

"Oh, Ben…"

"Shhh," he moaned against my ear, sending shivers raking down my spine. He withdrew slightly and tensed as he returned again, and again, and again. Each thrust sent my head spinning.

This was what I needed. *Him*. I needed *him*. Every second felt real, natural, like it was meant to be. And the world disappeared as Ben made love to me for hours until I collapsed in his arms and slipped into the deepest, empty sleep.

***

Water, it was everywhere.

I was utterly emersed in the cold depths of the sea as whorls of light danced around me. The way I just floated in place and the annoying tug at the edges of my vision assured me this was just another dream. But something nagged in the back of my mind.

This is a memory.

My arms drifted outward, and I noticed how small they were. I kicked my little legs, bolting for the surface that seemed to never come, but the bright light of the sun was like a beacon, and I fought to reach it.

Just as my fingertips breached the surface, something grabbed my ankles and pulled me back. I glanced down, and my heart tightened with panic. A siren's horrific clawed hands wrapped around my legs, refusing to let me go, and she grappled at my pajamas, crawling up my body until her otherworldly silver eyes stared into mine, and she opened her mouth to reveal a set of pointed teeth.

A gurgled, wet scream erupted from me, letting water pour into my lungs, filling my body, as did some strange silvery essence that seeped from the beast's mouth. I pushed her away and fought for the surface. When cold air touched my face, I sucked in a deep breath and pulled myself to the shore, where I collapsed on the moonlit sand, spewing the sea.

Suddenly, I was standing over the scene, staring down at my younger self…and I remembered. I watched the memory play out, knowing exactly what would happen as little Audrey sat up and unfurled her hand to reveal a small brown pouch. She grinned with delight as she triumphantly looked out over the water, the moonlight highlighting the soft features of her face as she turned and stared right at me.

My hand went to my throat with a gasp.

"It's ours now," she said in a layered, musical voice.

I slowly shook my head. "What have you done…."

Little me opened the bag and dumped a big, red pearl into her palm before tilting her head to show me glowing silver eyes. I stumbled backward into the grass, and as my body hit the ground, I bolted up in bed with a startle.

Sweat covered my skin, and I still wore my father's leather trench coat over a half-naked body. Ben's giant limbs draped heavily over my waist and legs as he snored deeply. I sat there for a moment, waiting for my breaths to calm down, focusing on slowing my racing heart while my brain struggled to accept the realization that had just occurred.

As a kid, I stole something from a siren and blocked out the memory ever since. But some parts were still muddy. Like why they called to me each night before that and why my eyes seemed to glow like moonlight.

I had to return the pearl and end all of this.

Ever so carefully, I peeled Ben's arm and leg off me and quietly slipped out of bed. I scooped my black jeans from the floor and tip-toed to my old bedroom as I clumsily hauled on my pants. He couldn't know. No one could know. All these years, all this shared guilt amongst my family…the burden I'd put on my grandmother.

It was all my fault.

Every step I took toward my bedroom caused a loud moan in the old floorboards, and I hunched my shoulders, hoping Ben wouldn't wake. Ever so carefully, I shut the door behind me and spun around to face the dark room. I flipped on the light and stared down at the worn hardwood, trying to remember which one I used to hide things under. I thought I was so clever, nicking things from people and finding treasures on the beach to hide away in my secret stash. But it'd been almost two decades, and I'd long forgotten all about it.

I stepped around the room, putting pressure on each floorboard until I felt one that was looser than the rest. My nail beds protested as I pried up a two-foot-long piece and set it aside. Shells and rocks with geodes, bits of Mom's jewelry, gems and coins from Nan's collections; what a little sleepwalking thief I was. There was even a small dagger.

I pulled it out of the dusty space between the joists, and it made a *schwing* sound as I slid it from the black leather sheath for a second. And there, sitting just as I remembered it…the little brown satchel. Before I could talk myself out of it, I stuffed the bag into my pocket and the dagger in the other before heading down to the dark beach behind my nan's house.

The water was calm and eerie, and moonlight looked like a silvery spilled over its surface. Inside the deep pocket, my hand clenched around the bag.

"Sirens!" I called out, feeling silly. I had no idea how to summon them. They'd always called me. I waited a moment, but nothing happened, so I took a step closer to the shore. "Beasts! I have something you want!" I pulled out the bag and dangled it in the air. "Come and get it, or I'm tossing it in the sea."

My breath burned in my chest in wait. Just as I was about to give up, something bubbled on the water and floated toward me. An iridescent head with two terrifying, almond-shaped black eyes blinked at me curiously.

"It would not be wise to submit a siren's pearl to the sea, Audrey Cobham," its layered musical voice carried through the air without a mouth in sight. "Didn't your mother warn you about wishes?"

"My name is Audrey White."

The beast rose a few more inches, its watery form slowly taking on solid colors and textures as it dried in the cool night air. "Call yourself whatever you like. You're still a Cobham by blood."

Anger toiled in my gut, and I thrust my arm out, offering the satchel. "Here, I took this from one of you when I was just a kid. I didn't know any better. Take it and leave me alone. Stop haunting my dreams."

The siren sniffed at the air and tilted her head adorned in strings of shells and bone. "A blood pearl?" A cloudy film blinked over its massive bug-like eyes. "You cannot return a blood pearl, girl."

"But I stole it."

"You did not."

"Yes, I *did*," I replied impatiently. I opened the bag and dumped the large pearl into my hand. "Your kind haunted me every night, hypnotizing and luring me to the water. So, I took it one night. I remember now."

"You remember wrong. A blood pearl is given, not taken."

"Why would it be given to me?"

She rose even further, standing on legs beneath a thick

seaweed curtain that fanned around her like a dress. It dragged over the sand, and I stood in frozen horror as the creature walked toward me.

"We gift our sisters all sorts of things."

I shook my head. "I-I'm not your sister, though. I'm a human being."

She sniffed at the air around me and flicked her tongue out with a wet sound. "Some still remain, yes. I can taste it in the air."

"Some of what?"

Her face twisted, and her toothy mouth curved in a wicked grin. "Your humanity."

My stomach soured. "Excuse me?"

Those otherworldly eyes flitted over me as if seeing something for the first time. "Oh…" She leaned back with a smug look. "You don't remember." My blank and horrified expression had her cackling softly to herself, and she gently caressed the line of my jaw with a pointed fingertip, sending a cold shiver down my back. "The wish you made."

"What?" But as I said the word, the truth filled me. The dreams, the nightmares, the silvery eyes, and the way the sea always screamed in my head. I shoved at her chest and stepped away, tears tightened my throat, and I shook my head in disbelief. "You can't accept wishes from *children*! That's not fair!"

She waved her hand from side to side. "Fair, right,

wrong–" In a blink, she turned to water and sank into the sand, only reappearing behind me. I spun around. "Those human concepts mean nothing to us. Seneca foolishly befriended you and gave you a wish pearl. After a glimpse of our world and what we can do, you made a wish, and my sisters granted it."

My life replayed before my eyes; top grades, acceptance letters, scholarships, a dream career, sexual partners…I had always chucked it up to hard work and a bit of luck. All this time…it couldn't be…

My heart sank, and I shot a look toward the house. Did I attract Ben into my life? Was I able to lure the things I wanted…was he…

I closed my eyes and pushed the thought away.

"Take the pearl," I said through clenched teeth, thrusting the satchel at her. "And revoke the wish."

The siren's laugh came from all around, as if her voice was connected to her sisters of the sea, and they all took pleasure in my pain. "It does not work like that, Audrey Cobham."

"I don't want to be like you!" Tears spilled over. "Any little kid would wish to be a mermaid, princess, or some kind of beautiful, magical thing! Take it back!"

"You say we're beautiful, yet you reject the gift we've bestowed upon no one before you."

Rage simmered below the surface of my skin as my

fingers wrapped the dagger's hilt in my pocket. "A storm can be beautiful. An erupting volcano can be enchanting. It doesn't make them any less horrific."

"You wound me with your words."

I moved swiftly without breaking our locked stare, and her obsidian eyes went wide as I lodged the dagger in her chest. Her slimy hands gripped my arms, and I pulled her closer, twisting the knife.

Our noses almost touching, I said spitefully, "No, I wound you with my blade."

The horrified expression on her face melted away and morphed into a look of pure evil as she glanced down and wrapped her hands around mine, pulling the dagger free. Sea water spilled from the wound.

"I am not made of mortal flesh and bone, silly girl." She collapsed and soaked into the sand again, reappearing a few feet to my right. "But I admire your tenacity." She mocked contemplation, clucking her tongue in a very human-like way. "I'll offer you a trade."

My grandmother's words rang in my ears. "I know better than to make a deal with your kind."

"*My* kind?" Her half-watery form floated over the sand as a set of gills in her neck moved with a deep breath, and I wondered if she truly needed to breathe when on land. "Do not forget what magic flows in your blood, Audrey Cobham. My kind *is* your kind, whether you believe it or not."

"Then I'll go back to the mainland, as far away from the sea as I can."

She cocked her head. "And what good did that do you all these years? The call of the sea may have been quieter, but it still lived within you every night. Try as you might. You cannot run away from what you are." My hand shook as I gripped the dagger, unsure of what to do. "It would be in your best interests to accept my offer."

I gritted my teeth. "What's the offer?"

"A game," she replied, pacing circles around me. "Go to the past and find a way back with the help of old friends, but you cannot tell them who you really are."

"You're insane."

"If you play the game successfully, I'll revoke your foolish wish."

I stole another glance toward the house. Ben and my family would wake up tomorrow to find me gone. What would they do? Jump to conclusions? Get themselves killed trying to come and find me? "There has to be another way."

"There is not."

"Can't I just trade the blood pearl? Take it and leave my family and me alone." She just shook her head, knowing she'd backed me into a corner. "What's to stop me from tossing this thing in the sea and wishing for every one of your kind to drop dead?"

Her dark gaze fell to the bag in my other hand. "A blood pearl is not for wishes, silly girl."

I threw the bag at her and turned toward the house. "Go to hell, then."

As I walked away, she called after me, "Was that a wish I heard?"

I spun around. "What? No–"

"I distinctly heard a wish," the siren said, a fresh white pearl gleaming between her fingertips.

"No, I didn't–"

The beast released a piercing wail, and water rose around her in a monstrous tornado before twisting in my direction. Eyes wide with fear, I took off running for the house, but it was too late. The sea came crashing down over me, seizing my limbs, dragging me back, and I was helpless to escape.

I kicked and screamed to no avail. The moon disappeared, and oxygen squeezed from my lungs as my vision darkened and my body gave up. I had no choice but to let the sea take me into the abyss as the distant laugh of the siren cackled in my ears.

And I was gone.

CHAPTER SEVEN

The loud, annoying caw of nearby seagulls startled me awake, and I peeled my face from the wet sand. Every inch of my body protested as I moved, and the blaring mid-morning sun had already set to work baking my skin.

I rolled over onto my back with a groan and realized my shirt still hung wide open, exposing my bare chest and black lacey bra. It was still half-soaked and filled with sand. Something dug into my side, and I shifted to adjust the big leather coat I wore and remembered the dagger in my pocket.

I bolted upright and craned my head from side to side.

To my left, the beach stretched as far as the eye could

see and continued around the bend of a small alcove. To my right, it led to a small town far in the distance. The tops of houses and smoking chimney stacks poked up from behind small foothills like pickets on a fence.

And, suddenly, everything came rushing back to me.

"Fuck!" I punched the sand around me. "Fuck, fuck, *fuck!*" I jumped and ran to the water, soaking my pants up to my knees. I kicked and punched at the sea, cursing it in pure, undiluted anger until my throat ran raw. "You stupid bitch! Take me back! I didn't ask for this!"

As if in answer, the shallow water violently pushed me back to the beach, and I stumbled backward onto my tailbone. I fisted sand and shells and threw them at the receding tide, but it gently rushed back to me and left the small brown bag that held the blood pearl.

I grabbed it and chucked it back to the sea, but it just came rushing back again. I swiped it and stood up, my blood pumping hot and heavy.

"Fine!" I spat. "I'll play your stupid game. But I'll win and find a way to destroy every last of you fucking beasts. Consider this a promise." My eyes narrowed at the sparkling sea. "Eternity is over. Your days are fucking numbered."

I collected myself and took stock of everything. I had no idea when or where I was, but it wouldn't be hard to figure it out once I reached that town in the distance. I glanced down at my bare chest and very modern clothing, all except for my father's baggy pirate jacket.

I wrapped it over my body like a bathrobe and secured it with the leather sash tied at the back. I checked every pocket and found my dagger, a handful of loose coins—unknown value—and a small compass. The needle told me north was directly out to sea, but that still didn't give me an idea of where I was.

"Okay, Audrey," I said to myself. "You can do this. Treat it like a job. Make a list, plan it out." My nerves slowly began to calm, and I slipped into a comfortable mode. This was a game, and I refused to lose.

The siren said I had to find a way back to the future with the help of old friends, but I couldn't tell them who I really was. I knew I'd need to secure some lodging, food, and possibly transportation. But the few coins I had couldn't possibly get me far.

But I wore a tennis bracelet that contained a couple dozen black diamonds, and my ears hung with ruby droplets—a Christmas gift from my parents a few years ago. I removed my jewelry and sat on a rock, prying each gem from the modern metal claws with the tip of my knife. I added them and the coins to the satchel that held the blood pearl and headed off for the town.

It was bigger than I thought, with a busy port full of ships, a bustling seaside market, and stone-laid roads that led to all the roads and main streets. I casually strolled through the tents and tables of vendors selling goods, everything from fresh fish to handmade treasures.

Discreetly, I watched and listened to a transaction as I pretended to peruse some spices and learned that the gold coins I had were called escudos, and there were silver ones, too, called reales. The merchant sold several sacks of grain, spices, meats, and butter that the person had stacked on a wooden trolly and only paid a couple of silver coins. I hoped that meant my gold ones would get me far.

I spent the afternoon walking around the market and port, absorbing everything I could by eavesdropping and watching. There was a good mix of dialects; English, Spanish, and some French. I could get by with all three and breathed a sigh of relief. It didn't take long to learn exactly where I was, either, and I wasn't sure if it was some cosmic joke led by the sirens or if this was exactly where I needed to be to find "old friends".

I was in Nassau. The heart and soul of the age of piracy. An unlawful playground for pirates, thieves, and murderers, and from the way the island port burst with life and activity, I could confidently guess it was early to mid-seventeen hundreds. And, if my goal was to find old friends, my parent's epic adventure must have already taken place.

The heart of the town consisted of some small shops, a baker, pubs, and a brothel. The sign above the chipped, teal-colored door claimed it to be Mademoiselle Aveline's

Inn & Menagerie, but the beautiful, busty women lounging over the edge of metal balconies told me it was more than just a place to rest my head.

I entered the brothel and tried to hide my distaste at the heavy stench of sweat and ale poorly covered by flowery perfumes. Patrons were tucked in dark corners, a beautiful lady draped over their laps as they drank from large mugs. An older woman with too much blush and a neatly pinned updo braided her lace-gloved hands as she approached me.

"Bonjour," she said, eyeing my bare, sand-covered feet. "Puis-je vous aider?"

"Do you have a room available?" I asked.

She sized me up and down. "Oui, for just yourself?"

"Yes."

"Do you require company?" Her English was impressive.

I shook my head. "No, I'm just staying a few days."

"Follow me." She crooked a finger over her shoulder as she turned for the front desk, and I walked closely behind, mindful of the scattered men, feeling their watchful stares. She plucked a key from a hook on the back wall and handed it to me. "The cost is two escudos per week. Your room is on the top floor, end of the hall, and you'll be provided one meal each day." Her crow's feet creased as she narrowed her eyes. "The cost doubles if you use the services of my girls. Comprenez vous?"

I nodded. "Yes, thank you."

"My name is Mademoiselle Aveline." She gestured toward a staircase near the back. "Do not bother my patrons; they shall not bother you."

I arched a brow. "You sure about that?"

Aveline gave me a look that said, *I dare you to test me.* "I'll have someone bring fresh towels and clean water to your room."

I left it at that and headed up the stairs, making a mental note to keep my stay as short as possible. I guess manners and hospitality were saved for the greasier clients who paid big coin for a full-service experience.

The room was small but housed a bed, table, two chairs, and a fine three-drawer dresser. The little balcony overlooked the bustling square below and let in a welcome breeze from the nearby ocean as I sat on the bed and collected my thoughts.

If I had to find old friends, that could be anyone. My parents knew a colorful bouquet of people from this time, stretched over half of the world. Would I have to sail for months to get to Scotland? Stay put and wait until someone familiar comes into port?

I glanced down at my attire, thankful my father's jacket covered almost everything, but realized that anyone who knew my parents would likely recognize the coat. The only stipulation the siren gave me was that I couldn't tell them who I was.

I had to get the jacket altered and acquire some clothing.

A knock came at the door, and I opened it to find a beautiful young girl with loose red curls and a smattering of freckles across her nose, a tray stacked with off-white towels, and a ceramic basin of water in her slender arms. She said nothing as she set the tray on the dresser, and I just stared; she couldn't have been older than fifteen.

"Uh, thank you," I told her, and she just nodded and headed for the door. "Wait." The girl turned to me, brows raised. "Could I bother you for some information?"

"Of course," she replied in a Welsh accent. "How can I help you, Miss?"

"Please, call me…." I swallowed dryly. There was no way I could give my real name here. "Ace. Call me Ace. I hoped to buy some new clothes and a pair of boots."

"There's a couple of boutiques in the square," she said. "I could show you."

I couldn't risk being exposed any more than I have until I looked the part and hid the fact that I was wearing the jacket of a very famous pirate. "If I gave you coin, could you perhaps buy me an outfit? Nothing fancy, just a pair of…trousers and a shirt." I glanced down at my dirty feet and then at her sandaled ones. "And a pair of boots? We look to be about the same size."

She gave an awkward courtesy. "Of course, Miss Ace."

"And it's just Ace, no Miss," I told her, but that seemed to make her nervous. "Or whatever you wish to call me."

She just bowed her head. "I'm needed in the kitchen for the afternoon," she admitted. "But I can deliver your new clothes this evening."

"Great."

The girl left the room, and I closed the door. I thanked the heavens there was a lock and ensured it was secured before I removed my damp jacket and jeans. I wrapped myself in a sheet from the bed and sat on the shallow balcony to people-watch for the rest of the afternoon, to try and soak up the lingo and how people behaved here.

But mostly, I was searching for a familiar face.

When the girl returned, a purple haze had cast the square below in twilight. She entered my room with a larger tray stacked with a pile of clothes, a pair of black boots, and a bowl of stew with a bun next to it. She noted the sheet I'd fashioned into a toga and gave me a peculiar look.

"My clothes were too wet," I said, and she just nodded as she eyed my torn plaid shirt. I didn't even think to hide it; a fabric and pattern like that wouldn't even exist here.

She set the tray down on the bed. "Well, I do hope these new garments will serve you better," she replied and picked up the shirt Ben had shredded between her fingers, letting it dangle as she examined it.

I quickly swiped it away and balled it up with my skinny

black jeans. "Thanks, I really owe you." I pulled the drawstring open on my bag. "Oh, I should have asked earlier, but is there a tailor in town?" I gestured at my obviously overside jacket. "Normally, I would get a new coat, but this one belonged to…someone important to me. I'd like to keep it but have it more fitted to my size. Maybe even add some embellishments?"

She had a thoughtful look about her. "No, Miss Ace, I'm sorry. Nassau's only tailor just left for the Americas a few weeks ago. But my mother was a seamstress. I can sew. Perhaps I could help."

"Would you?" I jiggled my little bag of treasures. "I can pay you extra–"

She covered my hand with hers, shushing me as she pushed me further into the room. "Don't let Mademoiselle Aveline hear you." The girl cast a nervous glance at the open door. "She doesn't let us accept extra coin."

My heart hurt for this poor girl who was obviously sold into this life. I wondered where her mother was she spoke of.

I lowered my voice to a whisper. "Are you in danger here?"

The girl let out a quiet, manic laugh, and I saw the fear in her eyes. "Miss Ace, I'm an unwed, virgin orphan with no friends, no family, and no prospects. I was sold into slavery and purchased by Aveline a mere month ago for a *pretty penny*, as she calls it. Danger is everywhere. I'm a rare fawn in a forest full of hunters, and my master will only let the highest bidder shoot me."

Feminine rage boiled inside me, but I had to keep myself in check and remind myself where and *when* I was. "What's your name?"

"Kiri, Miss."

"Well, Kiri," I said. "How about I pay you in some other way?" Her puzzled, worried look kept me talking in a whisper. "You help me, and I'll help you."

"Help me with what?" she whispered back.

"I'll get you out of here."

Her eyes widened in a mix of horror and disbelief. "If you can truly get me off this god-forsaken island, I'll be indebted to you for the rest of my life."

I grinned, seeing my plans fall into place. I didn't know this island, and I didn't know these people. My only hope of locating anyone from my parent's past was to have someone like Kiri by my side.

So, I got dressed in the clothes she brought—a pair of grey pants and a loose cream-colored blouse clearly meant for a small man, but it fit me perfectly. I shoved on the leather boots and slipped a single ruby into my pocket before descending the stairs to the lively tavern below.

The setting sun brought along three times as many male patrons as I had seen before, all much louder and far drunker than I could stand. I swerved in, out, and around their tables, my eyes scanning for Mademoiselle Aveline. I found her in a far corner, encouraging one of her girls to sit on a man's lap. I tried to hold an indifferent look as I neared. When she noticed me, her cheerful expression turned stonily as she met me halfway.

"What can I do for you, Miss?" she said. "Are the quarters to your liking? How about the stew? People come from all over the island to taste Kiri's cooking."

"It's all wonderful, thank you," I replied and cleared my throat. "May I have a word with you in private? I'd like to discuss some business."

She seemed surprised but nodded and swept an arm, an invitation toward a door behind the front desk. Aveline led me to what looked to be her office, paisley walls adorned with shelves of leatherbound books and odd trinkets that appeared to be from every corner of the world. Being a Madam, she surely crossed paths with all sorts of people that came to the island.

She lit a cigarette and sat on the edge of her desk. "What is it I may do for you?"

"I'll be in town for a few days, at the very least, and I'd like the aid of an assistant. Someone to show me around, guide me about the island, and run errands."

Eyes circled in heavy kohl glanced me up and down with distaste. Why did she seem to hate me? "I can arrange for one of my girls to join you for the week." She tapped the ash into a glass tray. "But it'll cost you."

"I have no doubt," I replied. "But I would like to request Kiri, if I may."

"Kiri?" she balked and doused the cigarette's tip as she stood up.

"Yes, I understand she's new and a virgin, and I'd prefer not to take away from your usual selection of girls." She crossed her arms beneath a silken kimono, eyeing me curiously. She knew what I meant; I didn't want someone already trained by her to sniff out ways to take advantage of me.

She gave me a challenging look. "You don't understand. Kiri is my rare gem."

I fished out one of my rubies and offered it to her. "Well, a rare gem for a rare gem seems like a fair exchange, then." Her eyes lit up. "Don't you think?"

Aveline chewed at her lip momentarily as she stared at the ruby. Finally, she sighed. "You won't touch her virtue?"

I shook my head. "No, I swear. I just need her as an aid." *Then I'll be helping her escape you.*

"You know, when you first waltzed in my door, barefoot, wet clothes hanging off you, I assumed you'd been a stowaway on one of the ships, looking for refuge. When you asked to talk business, I figured you were asking me for work."

I held an indifferent smile, but inside I was dying to

claw her eyes out. "Appearances can be deceiving."

"En effet." Aveline pinched the gem between her fingers. "Very well, Kiri is yours for the week. Is there anything else I can help you with?"

I was about to say no, but then I remembered. "Actually, there is."

A short while later, I returned to my room, where Kiri waited on the balcony, my brown satchel clutched in her hands. She bolted to her feet and shoved the bag at me.

"You really shouldn't leave this lying around, Miss Ace. You cannot trust anyone here."

I set down the basket of sewing supplies Aveline gave me and shut and locked the door. "Can I trust you?" Without hesitation, she nodded, and everything in me believed her. She reminded me so much of Evelyn. "Good, because I just paid Aveline to let me have you for the entire week."

She seemed to stop breathing as she scanned my face for any sign that I was lying, and a heavy sob erupted from her as she wrapped both arms tightly around me.

I patted her back. "Shh, it's okay. I promised, remember? You help me, and I'll help you. Consider this your last day doing…." I cringed, "whatever Aveline makes you do outside of the kitchen."

Kiri pulled away and wiped the tears from her moss-colored eyes. "Thank you."

I picked up the basket of thread and needles. "Thank

me later. We've got work to do."

Kiri measured me and then pinned the jacket around my body. She worked well into the night as I sat on the bed, and we talked about her life. She grew up in a tiny village in Wales. Her home was ransacked by pirates, her family was killed, and she and her brother were sold into slavery. She came to Nassau on a ship with a few others. They were auctioned off to work for Madams or as chambermaids in some high houses.

I asked her how much she knew about the port.

"It's a small island. Word travels easily," she said as she attached some part of my jacket to the back. "What would you like to know?"

"What ships have come in recently?"

"It's been a busy week." She thought for a moment. "There have been several cargo ships, but they come here on a regular route every month or so. The tailor left on the Adventure Galley."

"Any still in port right now?"

She hummed and hawed as she sewed the most beautiful craftsmanship into my father's jacket. "Captain Avery's Fancy came in yesterday. The Royal Fortune's been docked for a few days now." She trimmed some threads and eyed her work before moving on to another piece of the jacket. "Oh, and The Queen's been here for a few days, as well. But I hear they're set to sail tomorrow."

My heart skipped a beat. "What did you say?"

"The Queen," she repeated and held up the finished jacket. "It's a gorgeous red beast that sits the furthest out to sea."

My heart fluttered with excitement. This was it. This was the lead I was looking for because The Queen…I knew it well; from the journal entries and the stories I grew up with. Kiri was right; it was a beautiful ship, a beast to be revered, one that sailed the seas and led many adventures for its crew…

A crew once captained by my mother.

CHAPTER EIGHT

With a better-fitting jacket and Kiri at my side, we slunk through the shadows of the port in search of The Queen. Half a dozen ships had pulled themselves close to the shore, but the red beast with yellow portholes sat further out, so far the crew would have had to row in. I remember reading in Mom's journal that they used to do that to prevent looters and thieves from boarding the ship.

"Do you know the captain and crew?" Kiri whispered as I found a small rowboat and craned my neck to ensure the coast was clear.

"Sort of," I replied. "It's a long story. They don't know me, but I need their help getting home."

"And where is home, exactly?"

I groaned as we shoved the heavy wooden dory into the water. "Far from here."

We rowed out to The Queen, and I was thankful I'd chosen the rowing machine at the gym every day for the last three years. My arms still burned, rowing the short distance, but at least the muscles weren't green.

Kiri needed no help climbing the ropes that hung from the groaning ship, even in a little cotton dress, and we scaled the side quietly, helping one another over the railing. The deck was dark aside from the scanty bit of candlelight that trickled out from the window in the captain's quarters.

"I don't believe anyone's here," Kiri whispered as we peered in the window.

"Good," I replied, sighing in relief when the door opened. "I need to figure out who the captain and crew are first."

The quarters smelled of rosemary and a faint tinge of metal. The way the bed was hardly more than a heap of linens and the shelves overflowing and disorderly told me the captain was likely a male, which didn't look good. Uncle Gus was dead, and Uncle Finn was running his family's keep in Scotland. Who captained my mother's old ship?

"What exactly shall I be looking for?" Kiri asked.

I skimmed through some old papers on the desk. "Anything that gives me a name. I need to know who runs this ship."

She perused a tall bookshelf near the door. "You know, Miss Ace, most pirates would behead anyone who dared trespass on their ship."

I looked through the drawers. Damn, this captain loved knives. There had to be at least a dozen or so tucked away in every nook and cranny. "Don't worry, if it's who I think it is—*hope* it is—they're not the type to behead without a damn good reason."

The door slammed shut, and the candle doused, shrouding us in darkness. "Then ye think wrong."

Shit. In the darkness, I heard Kiri scurry to my side and fumble around the desk. A pair of heavy boots took slow, taunting steps around the room.

"Now, what would two pretty wee things be doin' sneakin' aboard my ship at this hour?" the man asked.

Next to me, Kiri trembled, but I wasn't scared. I knew exactly who he was by his Scottish accent and sheer size of him. But he was supposed to be in Scotland. Uncle Finn was captaining The Queen?

"How about you light that candle and face us like an honorable man?" I challenged.

He chuckled darkly. "And who says I am the honorable type?"

"A hunch."

Silence filled the room, and I would have given anything to see his face, read his expressions, and gauge his demeanor. A few years had passed since my family and I left the past. Anything could have happened since. Maybe Uncle Finn wasn't the same loveable character my mother depicted him to be in her journal.

A match struck, revealing where he stood near the wardrobe to the left, and he lit an oil lamp hanging on the wall. Kiri gripped my arm and tucked in close. Finn stomped across the room and held the lamp just a few inches from our faces. He gave a once over to Kiri, but those deep green eyes lingered on me, scanning and searching.

Finally, he blew a grumble breath through his nose and grimaced beneath a burly red beard. "Yer not from around here."

I swallowed tightly. "No, I just arrived. This is my… friend, Kiri. We're in search of a ship looking for a few extra hands."

"Is that so?" He had a knowing look about him as he stepped back, holding his scrutinizing stare over us. He tipped his chin towards my friend. "Kiri, eh?" She nodded. "By the looks of ye, I wager yer Welsh?"

She nodded again. "Yes, Sir. Cymorthyn."

His bushy red brows rose. "Cymorthyn? The minin' town?" He shook his head, clucking his tongue. "Aye, I heard what happened. My condolences." Finn tilted his head and fixed his gaze on me with a half grin. "And ye? Where ye from, lass?"

Shit. I hadn't thought of a believable backstory. My mind raced for an answer, and I just blurted out, "Newfoundland."

He didn't move, didn't flinch or blink. "What the bloody Christ are ye doin' down here?"

I had to be careful with my words. The siren said I couldn't tell anyone who I really was. But I also knew I couldn't fabricate a string of lies. It'd be too hard to keep track of, and someone would surely catch on. I thought of every word.

"I was…taken against my will," I replied, my mouth running dry at the thought of giving too much away and ruining the morbid game the siren was playing. "And I was left here to fend for myself."

The space between his brows pinched together as he glanced back and forth between us. "Taken by whom?"

My mind crashed into a brick wall, and I held my breath. But it was Kiri who spoke.

"The same men who brought me here." She stepped in front of me. It was a bald-faced lie, and I faltered for a second but quickly steeled my expression. "She helped me escape, and we heard this ship was looking for a few crew members."

"Is that so?" Finn replied, taking three long strides

across the room to grab us both by the arms, shaking and yanking us close to his massive frame. His eyes flashed with delight. "Then let's pay a visit to the captain, shall we?"

***

Kiri and I were silent as Finn practically dragged us back to town and through the stone-paved streets to a small pub. All the while, I thought of two things; why did Kiri cover for me?

And who was the captain of The Queen?

Was it some murderous pirate that hired Finn to do his bidding? Was I going to have to try and convince Finn to help me while also fearing for my life? And what about Kiri? I'd promised to help her. I had to make sure whatever deals or situations I landed myself in on my quest to get home, I still kept my promise to help her escape.

The pub reeked of ale and cigars, blanketed in a musky layer of sweat and bad breath. In one corner, a fiddler played some jaunty tune. A few tables down the center were skirted by men playing cards. At least it wasn't the brothel.

With a firm grip on our arms, Finn wound through the crowd and headed for the back of the tavern, where the noise died off a bit. A gorgeous, pale woman with a heap of black curls pinned haphazardly about her face stood crossed-legged against the edge of a table while she picked at her nails with the tip of a dagger. Her bored eyes saw Finn and then flashed with dark delight at the sight of Kiri and I.

"Finnigan," she practically cooed, her voice like warm milk. "What have you brought me?" Every word curved with a slight accent. Scandinavian or something.

He released his grip and slung a giant arm over our shoulders. "New recruits."

The woman rolled her eyes as she folded her dagger in half and stuffed it in the pocket of her leather jacket. I noted the fabric roses tucked under the shoulder caps and how the garment seemed to be made perfectly for her slender, feminine body.

"That's disappointing," she replied and set a pair of deep purple eyes on us in almost a predatory way like a lion watching its food walk away. A shiver ran through me as she stepped aside, revealing a small blonde woman with sun-kissed skin sitting at the table.

"New recruits, you say?" the woman asked without looking up. Her downy waves fell loosely around her shoulders, partly covering the crisscrossed bandolier of knives. She wore a crisp white blouse, the poofy sleeves rolled up to her elbows, revealing more tanned skin. I immediately knew who she was. My mother's old friend, Lottie.

She didn't give Kiri a second look, but her pale blue

eyes looked at me curiously.

Finn collapsed in a chair, his long legs stretched across the floor. "Found them pokin' around the ship." I shot him an incredible look, and he just grinned with glee as he squirmed in his seat. Like a little kid, pleased at his dirty work.

Lottie rose and came around the front of the table, her eyes never leaving me. I only saw a sort of emptiness in them, a dried-up pain that only came with losing something bigger than ourselves. I remembered my mother's journal, the story of one of her best friends. A woman I called *Aunt*, even though I'd only met her once. I could only hope she didn't recognize me.

"Cynda, what do you think?" Lottie asked, finally dragging her stare away from me. "Do we need any help aboard the ship?"

"From trespassers? No, I don't believe we do." The scary woman sucked her perfect white teeth and cut a salacious grin at us. "But I'm sure we could find a use for them."

Lottie tilted her head at me.

Kiri cleared her throat. "I can cook and clean, Miss–Captain."

"Arrrg," Finn groaned and wiped the foam from his beard. A giant mug of ale had somehow appeared in his hand. "We need the help, and ye know it. Cillian just left, and Rhoda is dead." He rolled his eyes toward Cynda, who stood in a dark corner. "And not how ye be thinkin', either. Ye can find yer own help before we sail."

I studied Cynda, trying to keep my face cool and calm, but it was hard not to let my mind wander and panic rise. What sort of help did she need? Also, who was Rhoda, and how did she die? I squashed the churning feeling and exchanged a look with Kiri.

I sucked in a deep breath. "We just need to get off this island. We can be of use, I swear."

Lottie had a look of realization flit across her face. Two young women, alone on a lawless island. I just prayed she felt sorry for us. She seemed to struggle with her thoughts but blew out an exasperated breath.

"Do you have sea legs?" she asked us.

"Yes," we both replied together. While Kiri spent weeks on a ship to get here, it was a bald-faced lie for me. I'd avoided boats and water my entire life. But they didn't need to know that.

"What skills do you have?" Lottie continued to interrogate.

Shit.

Kiri brightened. "I can keep a ship clean all on my own and cook just about anything."

Lottie seemed impressed and then turned to me with a look of expectancy. She raised her brows and crossed her arms. "And you?"

My mouth opened, but no words came out as panic burned in my chest.

"Aye," Finn said, stomping as he clapped me on the back. I just about fell forward. "She looks like a strong lass; we'll put her to work on the deck."

Lottie didn't seem convinced. "Are you skilled with any weapons?"

Technically, I was a weapon myself. The words of my old sensei rang in my ears about using our skills for self-defense and never as a weapon to cause harm. But besides that, Nan let me play with her collection, and I'd spend hours on the deck, swinging and whipping it around. She showed me how to properly hold it and use it defensively. More like a shield than a weapon. I swallowed nervously but nodded.

"Yes, I'm experienced with a sword."

She scanned me up and down. "Where is it?" She rolled her eyes at my look of confusion. "Your *sword*."

"Oh, I…lost it."

She pursed her lips and thought momentarily before giving Finn a bored look. "They're your responsibility."

He gave a dutiful nod. "Aye, Captain."

Kiri and I exchanged a sigh of relief. Little did she know how crucial it was that we got on this ship. If the objective of the siren's game was for me to find my parent's old friends, I had two right here in front of me. This had to be the right path.

Or was it the siren's blood that ran through my veins, luring what I wanted right to me?

Finn clapped his giant hands together, startling me. "Then it's settled! Let's drink!" A bar maiden appeared with several jugs of ale, and Finn handed them out. "So, what do we call ye lasses?"

"My name's Kiri, Sir." She took a big gulp of her beer, and I wondered if she was old enough to drink. I suppose that didn't matter here. "Kiri Thomas."

His deep green eyes sparkled at me from over the rim of his mug. "Uh, Ace," I told them all. I couldn't give them my father's last name and definitely not my mother's last name. I couldn't risk them connecting the dots. "Ace…Sheppard," I finished as my grandfather's name sprang to mind.

I couldn't read her face, but she offered her hand to shake, and I took it. "Don't make me regret this."

***

Singing and dancing filled the bar as we sat in the back corner and drank mug after mug of ale. I didn't say a word, just watched and observed everyone's body language as they took turns playing darts—only instead of darts, they just threw small daggers at the wooden-clad wall.

Food appeared; an array of cheese and meats and baked goods. I peered into a giant iron pot of some kind of brothy soup. I poured a bowl and took a scoop of cheese as I sat off to the side. Kiri did the same and joined me.

After a few bites of stew, I nudged my knee against hers. "Why did you do that?"

She stuffed meat and cheese inside one of the buns and lobbed off a big bite. It bunched to the side of her mouth as she replied softly, "I figured it out pretty quickly, you know." I just gawked at her, appalled. How could she have possibly figured out I was from the future? She continued chewing for a moment. "The men's jacket, the bare feet. I get it. You're hiding from someone."

It took me a moment to consider what she was saying, so I ate with her in silence. She thought I was running from some man. I gave her a half smile. "Well, thanks anyway. It's nice to know I can trust someone."

Finn came stomping over in a non-threatening way. His clunky brown boots were wet from spilling his beer. But he didn't seem to care as he pulled up a chair. It screeched across the floor, and he plunked down in it.

"Ace and Kiri, eh?" We just nodded and finished up our food. He pointed at the scarily beautiful woman. "That's Cynda. Don't let the bitch scare ye. She's harmless." He tipped his head back and forth as if to say, *sort of.* "And ye ken the captain." He motioned to Lottie across the room.

She was conversing with two men, and they moved their arms as if they were giving directions.

"And what about you?" I asked.

His eyes locked on mine as if something clicked in place. "Finn. Finnigan Artair. Sailing master."

I couldn't look away; those eyes were ones I'd already known so well from my mother's stories and the descriptions of her friends. And a vague, cloudy memory of standing in a beautiful home in Scotland and my little hands getting lost in his giant mitts as he held me close and said goodbye. I wanted to tell him. I wanted to wrap my arms around his neck and thank him for everything he'd done for my parents.

Finally, he looked away as Lottie returned, one of the young men in tow. He looked somewhat normal, with short, sandy brown hair and a pair of wire glasses.

"And this is our other new recruit," Finn said, pointing to the small man. "Eric. Saved him from a burning ship in Jamestown. Good thing, too, because he–"

"We don't have time for bedtime stories," Lottie grumbled and motioned to Cynda. The woman retrieved her daggers from the wall and joined us.

Finn read Lottie's face and chuckled to himself. "You found it?"

"Yes, we leave at first light." Lottie had a determined look about her.

"Where are we going?" I asked, exchanging a glance with Kiri.

The captain smiled. "To get ourselves a marksman, an old friend named Benjamin Cook."

CHAPTER NINE

Sleep never came.

I couldn't stop thinking about the fact that, in a few hours, I'd be face-to-face with Ben. But not the Benjamin Cook I knew…no, not *my* Ben.

What would he be like? Would he be the same or completely different? How do I get on a ship with him and not act like we didn't have sex just days ago?

How do I pretend to not be in love with him?

Kiri slipped a few of her belongings to my room in the quiet hours of the night, and we hid them with my stuff—which wasn't much—in a large leather shoulder bag, she'd picked up for me when I gave her money to buy me some clothes.

Aveline might notice if Kiri walked out in the morning with her own belongings, but she couldn't say anything to me, a guest. I lay on my bed and stared out the window, waiting for the crack of bluish-purple over the horizon.

Kiri slept next to me, a picture of her brother clutched in her hands. I jostled her shoulder, stirring her from her peaceful slumber, and her green eyes pried open with a yawn.

I smiled. "It's time to go."

The brothel was eerily quiet as we crept downstairs, and Kiri didn't give it a second glance as we exited to the empty street out front. I may be secretly searching for a way back to the future, but she was fighting for her life, narrowly escaping a fate at the hands of men, and braving an unknown world in search of her brother. She had more courage in one finger than I ever possessed. I admired her.

Just as planned, Finn waited for us at the end of a path that seemed to lead away from town. He sized us up and down and arched a thick, russet brow.

"Packing light?"

I shrugged; the weight of my bag was barely noticeable. "We don't need much."

It seemed Kiri had almost as few belongings as I did. A knitted shawl, a hairbrush, a second dress, and one extra pair of undergarments. I didn't comment on it as she smuggled them into my room the night before, but I told myself I'd use some of my treasure to buy her new clothes the first chance I got.

A few minutes later, Lottie and Eric showed up on horseback, with two other horses trailing close behind as they held the reins.

"Where's Cynda?" Kiri asked.

"She sleeps during the day." Finn took the smaller brown horse and handed me the leather reins of a larger white mare. "Ye two will have to share."

I thanked the heavens my father taught me how to ride a horse. I hopped in the saddle with ease, pretending not to notice the surprised look from the big Scotsman, and extended an arm to Kiri to hoist her up behind me.

We rode for a few hours until Nassau disappeared from behind, and a sprawling countryside spanned around us. All the while…my stomach was in knots. We were on our way to see Benjamin, and I had no idea how to act around him. The siren was very clear; find my parents' old friends, but do not tell them who I was.

I decided my best chance was to stay as quiet as possible and limit my interactions with him. I still had no idea how to use their help to get back home. It wasn't like I could just come out and ask. Maybe their next mission aligned with mine and would lead me to a means of time travel. Or perhaps the siren would just appear once I reached a certain point.

There were several ways to travel through time, that much I knew, but they all required a wish or magic of some kind. Touching the water where the sun and moon meet on the surface, using a siren's pearl, getting a witch to enchant an item from the time you wanted to go to.

The witches, the Keepers of Time, could open portals and send me home, but I had a feeling the siren would do everything in its power to prevent me from doing that. I didn't just stumble back in time. This was a game, and I had no choice but to play.

The only clue I had was the strange pearl in my pocket. The siren refused to take it back, said she couldn't accept it and that it wasn't for wishes. It was called a blood pearl. Perhaps, if I figured out what blood pearls were for, it would lead me to the next step in the game.

A small farm appeared in the distance, nestled at the foot of rolling hills. As we neared, I could see sheep and pigs meandering about their pens, chickens basking in the sun, and endless rows of gardens sprouting green tops of various vegetables.

We stopped at the gate to a wooden fence of dried logs surrounding most of the property and tied the horses before following Lottie into the garden. I hadn't noticed a man hunched over a garden bed, his hands sifting through the soil.

I swallowed dryly and wrung my clammy hands together as I watched him stand up. I'd know the shape of him anywhere, and my heart raced in my chest as he spun around. But it wasn't the loving, lighthearted face I'd recently fallen in love with. No, gone was the light of life from his brown eyes, an empty look of boredom in its place.

Ben wiped the dirt from his hands and narrowed his eyes at Finn and Lottie. "Long time no see."

Lottie put both hands on her hips. "It's good to see you, Ben." She glanced about the farm. "Domestication looks good on you."

There was a strange tension between them that I couldn't quite read, and I couldn't ignore the way his eyes passed over me as if I were a stranger. I suppose I was, to this Ben, anyway. A sharp pain twisted in my heart.

"Rich people love to eat," he replied with a hint of sarcasm in his sad voice. "And it's good to feel needed."

Finn stepped closer. "Nah, we needed ye aboard The Queen, and ye knows it."

Ben rolled his eyes and released a tired sigh. "Your captain seemed to think otherwise."

"I never told you to leave, Ben," Lottie chimed in, adding to the simmering tension between the three of them.

I held back with Kiri and a silent, observing Eric. I wondered then what part he played in the crew. He was a tall man but slender. I couldn't see him being a deckhand,

and Kiri would take the role of ship's maid and cook. He looked like he belonged in a dusty library somewhere, not sailing the seas with a bunch of pirates.

Ben chortled. "No, but you made it clear you were sick of me."

"The only thing I was sick of was your constant moping!" Lottie paused and took a deep breath, willing herself to calm down. "Look, you're family, Ben. And we need your help."

"No."

"No?" she repeated. "That's it? Just *no*? You haven't even heard what I have to say."

"Let me guess," Ben said with annoyance. "Another treasure hunt and another dead end. You still chasing the same hopeless dream, Charlotte?" Lottie pursed her lips in response, and Ben chuckled as he shook his head. "And you have the nerve to tell me I was moping. Look at you, desperately pining for a dead man."

"Watch yer tongue, boy," Finn warned steadily.

Ben straightened, his eyes darkening. "And *you* watch who you're calling *boy*. I'm old enough to be your grandfather."

That's right. Ben had been stuck aboard a cursed ship for over a hundred years before my mom and her crew saved him. Kiri gave me a puzzled look, and I pretended to be as confused as she was.

"It's different this time," she countered. Ben eyed her momentarily before glancing at Finn, who gave him a curt nod of assurance. "I know where the Endor Stone is."

"The Endor Stone is a myth."

It was hard to watch him like that; he had no smile, no bright or eager eyes. I ached to reach out and touch him. Another tidbit suddenly popped into my mind from the entries I'd read in Mom's journal. Ben's brother was the captain of their crew, a crew of pirates and treasure hunters.

Lottie grinned madly. "No, it's not a myth. It's real, and we're about to ship out and get it."

Ben seemed unsure, but I could see the contemplative look brewing behind his eyes. "How can you be so sure? The myth claims the stone was buried with the necromancer who created it."

"Aye," Finn drawled. "Solomon. A necromancer so evil and dangerous they had to encase him in stone and bury him at sea."

Lottie stepped closer, a sort of eagerness building in her stance. She was close to convincing him. "Ben, we know exactly where he's buried because his granddaughter is part of our crew. She's going to lead us right to it."

His brows shot up. "*Granddaughter?* Solomon existed thousands of years ago…." He stepped back and finally looked at Kiri and me, examining us with a disbelieving stare.

"She's not here," Lottie told him. "Cynda is a creature of the night."

"A *vampire?*" Ben exclaimed. "You dared invite a vampire aboard our ship?"

My blood ran cold, and Kiri let out a little gasp as she pressed against my side. Vampires, sirens, sea beasts. Did these things still exist in my time? How did they remain so hidden? But that explained so much about the mysterious and eerily terrifying woman I'd met the night before. Cynda was an actual vampire.

Ben began pacing in the dirt. "Anyone can touch the stone, but only another necromancer can use it. You know that, right?."

Finn and Lottie stepped aside and motioned to a quiet Eric. "Already taken care of. This is Eric. Fate had us cross paths a couple months ago during a quick stop in Jamestown, and it just so happens he's a practicing sorcerer."

Kiri and I exchanged a glance. What had we gotten ourselves into? Necromancers, sorcerers, vampires?

Ben nodded toward us in the back. "And what about them?"

I didn't trust myself to speak to him. Thankfully, Finn piped up. "Aye, deckhand and a cook."

He paced some more. "And what do you need me for, exactly?"

Lottie licked her dry lips. "The stone, it's protected by

magic but hidden in plain sight. It's also guarded by a sea monster, and we can't get close enough to hit the trigger that closes the beast's cage. We've…tried."

A somber feeling fell over them. Perhaps that's how the woman named Rhoda died. Ben stopped pacing and sighed.

"Ah, I see. And you need a marksman." When she nodded, he said, "No, I'm sorry, I can't, and neither should you. It's a suicide mission."

Lottie clenched her fists at her side. "Ben–"

"No, Charlotte," he replied quickly. "Stop chasing ghosts." He peered around at the five of us. "It's a long ride back. You can stay until morning, but then you have to leave."

***

We spent the rest of the day on the farm, exploring the perimeter, playing with the animals, and avoiding Ben. Well, I was avoiding Ben, anyway. Lottie went about with her discontented manner, pacing, and thinking. As the sun dipped behind the horizon, Cynda appeared on foot, and I didn't even want to know how she got there.

Finn kept an ever-watchful eye on Kiri and me, and Eric hardly interacted with anyone. I always spotted him slinking in a dark corner, a strange book clutched in his hands, watching and studying everyone with those wire glasses at the edge of his nose. A sorcerer? A real-life wizard? I tried to imagine the things he could do, but to me, he looked harmless. Normal.

Kiri was elated with her newfound freedom, and I tried to focus on that. Tomorrow, we'd be sailing on the ocean with a vampire, a sorcerer, and a couple of treasure-hunting pirates. But it was the sea that made my heart jump into my throat every time I thought of it. That, and the fact that the man I was falling in love with, was just a few yards away at any given moment.

Ben cooked up a giant pot of some sort of stew chocked with fresh veggies and lamb. I sat on the front patio with Kiri and ate two bowls in silence while the others gathered around inside and talked about old adventures.

I remained outside for the evening and watched as the moon replaced the sun in the sky. I couldn't go inside, couldn't bear to be around him for fear of what I might say or do. Even if we hadn't had the most mind-blowing sex of my life just mere days ago, Ben had still been my best friend for the last few months. I'd spent every waking moment with him; now, I was here, scared and unsure of what to do…all I wanted was to confide in him. But I was a stranger to the man inside the quaint little farmhouse.

As the night waned on, Kiri and the others found places to fall asleep, but I stayed outside and stared at the moon.

The sound of clunky boots, trying but failing to be quiet, approached from behind, and I waited as Finn appeared and sat down next to me on the step.

"Ye should get some sleep, lass. Big day tomorrow."

I shook my head as I chewed at the corner of my lip. "I can't sleep. God, I haven't slept in years. Not since…"

"Not since ye were a wee four-year-old?" His voice was soft and careful, and my head snapped up. Finn's deep emerald eyes sparkled with child-like wonder, and I could read it as plain as day on his face; he knew who I was.

Fear seared through my veins. "How–"

He spewed off some Scottish jargon and patted my knee. "Ye can change that jacket all ye like and watch yer words as carefully as possible, lass. But yer the spit right outta yer ma's mouth, Audrey. I knew it the moment the candlelight touched yer face." He thumbed over his shoulder. "Lottie knows it, too, but she willnae admit it. Won't face it."

The back of my throat tightened, and I wrung the edge of my father's jacket through my nervous fingers. "Do… do you think Ben knows?"

"Nah, that boy's too blinded by grief to see what's right in front–" I lifted my gaze and found another layer of realization on his kind face. His eyes searched as he tipped his head back. "Ah, so the bugger lived forever after all." He spewed off some more Scottish curses under his tongue.

"What sorta mess ye got yerself into, lass?"

I shook my head. "No mess. We…met a few months ago, and neither knew who the other was."

Finn chuckled lightly. "What's yer ma and pa have to say about it?"

I tipped my face to the sky and sucked in a deep breath, but it came out in a tired laugh. "Dad was surprisingly calm. Mom fainted."

He nodded contemplatively. "So, they lived happily ever after, did they?"

I smiled, tears forming around the rims of my eyes as I heard the love in his voice for his two friends and how he must have worried about all of us since we left so many years ago. "They did. They really did." Then a thought came to me. "Finn, how long ago did we leave? How much time has passed since my parents finally left these beaches?"

"Ah, time is a funny thing, isn't it? I look at ye and see a grown woman, but 'tis only been a mere seven years since Ben traded his soul for yer ma's. He sailed with us for a couple of years, treasure huntin', chasing Lottie's dark dream. But he was a ghost, and being at sea haunted him. So, Lottie cut him loose, told him to figure out what he wanted to do with his immortal life, because moping around her ship widnae do."

"What's her dark dream? What's with all this necromancing stuff?"

"Aye lass, we shoulda told ye more about the treasure we seek before recruitin' ye and Kiri," he replied. "We've all suffered great loss over the years, but none quite like Lottie. An unborn child, and then her husband. After we saved ye and yer brother from that bloody siren, Lottie stayed with my sister at the keep. But it didnae take long for her to discover the art of necromancing. She's been on a blind mission to find the pieces she needs to resurrect Augustus, and she's got one final piece in her sights."

"The Endor Stone?"

He nodded. "Aye. She carries his ashes in a jar and plans to resurrect Gus. I'm assuming ye knows who Augustus is?"

"Yes. Uncle Gus."

Finn nearly burst at the seams. "*Uncle* Gus? So…am I…"

I chuckled. "Yes, Uncle Finn." I gave a quick head tip toward the house. "Aunt Lottie. Little Charlie. Even Wallace."

"Bloody Christ," he replied and rubbed his beard over with a hand. "Ye ken the story, then."

"That I do." I chewed at my lip. "Except…Mom left out every detail about Ben. I'm only just discovering his part in all of it."

"Aye, what a tragic, twisted adventure. Curses and sirens." His brows shot up. "I assume those fuckin' beasts have somethin' to do with ye being here?"

My fingers trembled in my fists. I didn't know what to say, how specific the rules of the game were. "Yes."

Finn studied me momentarily and hummed to himself as he thought, his eyes locked on mine. "Cannae say much, eh'?" I didn't move. Didn't shake or nod, just stared and hoped he followed along. "Sounds like a threat of some kind." He smiled at the twitch from the corner of my mouth. "They gettin' ye to do somethin' to get home?"

My mouth gaped a bit as I carefully chose my words. "I'm not allowed to tell you who I am, but I need your help to get home."

He laughed and stretched his legs out over a couple of stairs. "Well, now, lass, lucky fer ye I know a bit about the fair folk, the sea fae." He waved a hand dramatically. "Even the woodland creatures. Magic is everywhere, Audrey, but 'tis immortal and full of loopholes, as well."

I stared at him puzzledly.

"What did the siren say? Word fer word."

I thought for a moment. "That I had to seek the help of old friends to get home, but I couldn't tell them who I really was."

He pointed a finger at me. "And there's yer loophole. Ye didna tell me anythin'. I just knew."

I let out a massive sigh of relief because he was right. He was so right. My grandmother often talked about the Fae and how they were their own worst enemies with their flawed rules and never-ending games.

Finn patted me on the back. "Dinnae worry, lass. I won't say a word, and we'll get ye home. I promise."

"Thank you."

He stood and towered over me. "We just have one thing to do first and may need yer help. We *need* Benjamin. That boy can knock the nose off a rabbit from a hundred and fifty feet away. Which…is roughly how close we can get to the lever that closes the kraken's cage."

"I thought you and my parents killed the kraken years ago?"

"Aye, I wish that were true. Sadly, there are kraken all over the ocean depths. Men have been capturin' them for centuries."

I wanted to avoid Ben as much as possible, but if getting him on that ship was my ticket to get home, I had to help. I swallowed noisily. "I'll…see what I can do."

He gave me a nod and said goodnight as he headed inside. Part of me was relieved that someone finally knew my secret and could possibly help me. But another part of me was riddled with worry. My Nan told me a lot about sirens and magic, and it was a fickle thing. I couldn't risk angering the siren, but I had to get home.

I stayed on the step, leaning against a post as the farm slept. Even though the ocean was nowhere to be seen, I could hear the waves crashing in the distance, and I wondered if we were close or was that the sound of the ocean haunting me?

I must have dozed off at some point. The sound of soft footsteps scuffed across the porch from behind. Ben sat down next to me without so much as a look and stared up at the pitch-black sky as he took a swig of rum straight from the bottle.

"Sorry, this is my spot," he said and paused. He handed me the bottle. "But I'm willing to share."

I gripped the neck of the brown jug and stared down into it for a moment. "Do you sit out here often?"

He finally looked at me, and I had to remind myself to breathe steadily. I just wanted to kiss away the pain. "Every night."

Benjamin was a rare beauty; wild chestnut hair, rosy lips, and eyes like two pools of chocolate. And part of me yearned to just reach over and touch him, just brush my fingertips over the tanned skin—so much darker than I knew him to be in the future. Of course, he practically lived outside in the sun here, tending to the animals and his garden. He was dirty from working and kissed by the sun.

I took a gulp of rum and relished how it warmed my veins.

"So, what's your story, Ace?"

My brows raised. "What do you mean?"

"Where did you come from? How did you get mixed up with that lot? Who's the young Welsh girl?"

I stumbled over my thoughts for a moment. I had to be very careful about what I said and the details I shared. "I…was brought here by my enemy and left to basically die if I don't find a way home. I met Kiri at the brothel I was staying at. She was recently–" I bit down the bile that rose. "Purchased to work there. So, I took her and fled, ran into Finn, and heard they needed help on the ship. So, we offered to join in exchange for a ride."

"That's awfully noble of you."

"What? The fleeing my enemy part or joining a crew of pirates?"

He chuckled lightly. "The part where you're risking your life to save that girl. If the madam finds out you're stealing one of her girls, she'll kill you."

My heart raced at the thought. "Well, I guess it's good we're sailing first thing tomorrow."

"I'm betting from how your face went ghostly white earlier; you had no idea you were sailing with a vampire," he said.

So, he was paying attention to me. I didn't remember his eyes even flitting in my direction at all. But my Ben was observant; I suppose this Ben would be, too.

I took another swig. "I had no idea vampires existed, let alone that Cynda was one."

A slight chuckle rolled through him, and it seemed labored. "And what part do you play in all this?"

"What do you mean?"

"Lottie only recruits people who are useful to her mission," he explained in a melancholy tone. "People who can sail, but also those with special skills."

I shook my head. "I'm just trying to get home and am grateful for the ride. I plan to help however I can, but there's nothing special about me."

"Where's home?"

I had to change the subject, so I conjured up a light chuckle and shook my head. "It doesn't matter. So, what's with this dark mission? Is Lottie truly going to resurrect someone?"

Ben took the rum from me and drank long and deep before wiping his mouth with the back of his hand. "Yes, and she'll stop at nothing. She's spent the last few years combing oceans, mountains, and deserts for relics and scrolls. She has everything she needs now, especially if this vampire can dive deep enough to open Solomon's grave."

I gnawed at my lip as I watched his movements. What an eerie thing to sit next to someone you know and care for, but they have no idea who you are. He was the same in every way and, yet, so different. That light, the almost tangible warmth that always radiated from him… wasn't there.

"Do you…do you think we can trust her?" I asked. His brows pinched together. "Cynda, the vampire. I mean, we're about to set sail tomorrow for who knows how long–"

"At least a few weeks," he said.

A few weeks at sea. My stomach churned.

"There you go again, turning white. You fear her that much?"

I swallowed nervously as he handed me the half-empty bottle, and I wet my throat as I cleared it. "I think I'm more nervous about being out on the water." I leaned in and jokingly whispered, "I may have oversold my abilities."

Ben laughed. A real one that didn't seem as forced, like it didn't have to crawl out from under a mountain of sorrow. "You know, you remind me of someone."

I flipped my hair over my shoulder. "Someone beautifully, obviously."

Another laugh rolled through him, and there it was. The light I missed. It was just a spark, but it was there for a quick second before he nodded to himself and stared down at the grass with a thoughtful look.

"Yes, very beautiful," he replied quietly. "And brave and fierce and loyal. She was everything the world should be but isn't."

My heart sank as I realized he was talking about my mother. After reading the journals, I knew he held a candle to my mother, but it was clearly more of a blazing torch. I was a fool.

I laughed it off and blinked away the wetness in my eyes. "Geez, no pressure." I handed back the rum.

"No, it's…it's not like that." Thoughts seemed to pain him. "I–there was a time when maybe it was, but I realized what I shared with her was different. I care for her as one cares for their soul." He pressed his hand over his heart, and he shifted to face me on the step, seemingly eager to purge the feelings from himself. "I spent a lifetime on a cursed ship doing unspeakable things for my brother. When I finally returned to the world, I found it had moved on without me, and I no longer recognized it. But…something in me recognized something in her. She made me feel like perhaps there was a place for me in this new world after all. I just had to find it." Ben shrugged–his shoulders lighter.

A comfortable silence draped over us as crickets chirped in the distance. My head swirled with rum and exhaustion, but it didn't matter. I could have stayed on that step with him forever. It'd only been a few days since I left the future, but I missed him. I ached to have him near, to laugh and eat with. To sit on Gertie at the end of a long day and bask in the warmth his presence offered. This Ben was no different. My soul still gravitated toward him, demanding to sit near that spark I loved so much.

Almost as if he had a siren's call of his own.

I nudged his knee with mine. "And? Have you found it yet?"

"Not yet." His chestnut eyes sparkled in the moonlight, but his half-smile failed to reach them. "But I have hope, and I promised her I'd spend my life searching for it."

It was almost painful to see him so…heart-rending.

This was a man who'd lost everything. His life, his family, and his friends. And now…he was all alone. Lottie was right, Ben was grieving, but it wasn't for the loss of my mother–yes, he was clearly sad and missed her–it was the loss of everything, even himself. He was like a child left alone in an unknown world.

But I had to convince him to come with us. Partly because I needed Lottie to finish her mission and partly because I worried maybe he was the *old friend* the siren spoke of. But mostly, I cared for him and couldn't bear to part with him, even if he had no clue who I was.

I patted his leg. "Well, I'm no expert, but I don't think you'll find it here, alone on a farm."

Ben stared blankly at my hand.

"Look, I can't force you to come," I said, and he tipped his head to the sky again. "I mean, you don't even know me. But I hardly know any of you. I'm just trying to get home, and they won't help me until this mission is done. Plus–" I shrugged and crossed my arms. "I could use all the help I can get on that ship."

He gave me a curious look. "What's the matter? Don't like boats?"

I stifled a startle. He'd said those exact words to me before, and their sound tickled my spine.

So, I replied the same. "No, I don't like water. I can't swim."

He gave it some thought, and I knew, part of me just *knew*, what he was going to say next because he'd told me before. It was like fate had inextricably bound us together in some way. I watched his mouth as it moved, knowing and waiting for each word to spill out.

"I'll try not to throw you overboard, then."

What twisted game was this? My stomach swirled, but I tried to seem relieved. "So, does that mean you'll come?"

"Well, how can I say no?" he replied, his eyes flitting to my reddening cheeks. "Besides, you don't know Lottie if you believe she would take no for an answer. I was just making her work for it."

There it was. More sparks. I could see it behind those dark brown eyes and his scruffy face, and I wanted nothing more than for that light to grow. I knew he loved the sea; it was part of him.

"So," I drank more rum and smiled at the man I was

falling in love with all over again. "Tell me about farming."

We stayed on the porch all night until the sun stained the morning sky. We talked about the farm animals and how he ran everything for hours. One of his cows was named Gertie, and I discovered that it was his mother's name. He showed me the barns and the fields, and I listened as he talked passionately about it all. This was a side to Ben I never knew, and I loved every moment of it.

We lazed about the porch, drinking rum, and he told me stories of his adventures with Lottie and the others. They encountered magic portals, ghost ships, and ninja pirates off the coast of China.

Sleep never came for either of us; it seemed the call of adventure had awakened something in both of us. I'd been terrified, confused, and worried before. But now, knowing Ben would be with me–even if he didn't know me–it made everything else seem so small.

So much for trying to avoid him.

CHAPTER TEN

I groggily opened my eyes as something nudged my leg, the morning sun warming my skin. I was on the porch, my face inches from Ben's. His giant hand hung heavily over the curve of my side, and I reached for his sleeping face to caress his beard–longer than he kept it in the future.

Someone cleared their throat, and I turned to find Kiri standing over us. She must have been the one to nudge my leg. Ben stirred and immediately pushed away as he sat up and straightened his thin linen shirt.

"We're about to leave," Kiri said, smiling between Ben

and me. She wore a long, off-white sweater, clearly hand-knitted, and gestured to Ben. "Is it okay if I borrow this?"

Ben just nodded.

I stood, rolling my eyes as I shoved at her arm and walked down the long porch toward the horses. We stood in an open patch of dirt as they trotted in place, eager to leave just as much as I was.

I turned to Kiri, and she had a shit-ass grin. "Don't," I told her, pacing.

She shrugged. "You two were awfully…comfortable this morning." Her sweet face was full of mischief. "And Benjamin was *particularly* comfortable." She raised her brows, and I couldn't help but chuckle.

Maybe *that's* what nudged my leg.

We waited there for a while until the sound of clunky boots on the patio had us both spinning around. Lottie, Eric, Finn, and Ben stalked toward us, bags and gear in hand. A sword swung from his side, and his brown coat hung heavy with whatever weapons and tools he had inside it. He completely avoided eye contact with me as he addressed the group.

"I've only got one spare horse." He threw a thumb over his shoulder. "My farm hand's staying here to run things, but he needs my second horse."

We all glanced around at the four horses we had brought. It was easy math; one of us had to ride with someone.

Kiri skipped toward the mare we rode in on. "That's alright, I can ride. Ace, you hop on with Benjamin."

I gave her a death stare, but she pretended not to notice. I spun slowly and only looked at him for half a second before swiftly swinging into the large saddle. Without a word, he climbed behind me and gripped the reins as I held onto the cantle.

We rode more than halfway back to Nassau without anyone saying a word. Ben fell to the back of the line as the horses slowed to a comfortable trot. I tried to focus on things; the blue sky, a passing bird, and my calculated breaths as I tried to ignore the fact that Ben's massive, warm body was pressed against my back.

I felt bad for being unable to avoid him. I thought I could play it cool and just hang out in the background while I found my way home. But it took me all afternoon to cave into his presence and open the floodgate to how I felt about him. Underneath it all…guilt ate away at me.

I was part siren, to whatever degree, and I wanted him. I wanted him so badly that it hurt. But was it the magic that flowed in my veins that attracted him to me? Was he helpless against the lure of a siren? According to my mother's journals, Ben had a long streak of bad luck with the beasts.

"You know, you could relax," he whispered deeply next to my ear, sending a shiver rocking through me.

I breathed and realized how wound I was; my back ramrod straight, fingers aching from still gripping the cantle. Slowly, I let my core disengage, and my back softened over his chest. Ever so slightly, his arms tightened, holding me in place.

His scruffy jaw brushed my temple. "I had fun last night. It was…nice."

I chuckled. "You don't sound so sure."

"Apologies. It's been a while since I stayed up drinking rum and singing to the sheep all night."

We laughed, and I turned just enough to look into his eyes. He stared at me for a moment, and then his gaze fell to my mouth. I wanted to close the few inches and put my lips on his–knowing what they already felt like, pillowsoft and warm, I yearned for it.

His breath hitched as he leaned in.

A loud whistle pierced the air, and I turned to find Lottie's stare cut down the line. She cocked her head to the approaching seaside port town up ahead. We were there. Now, one more phase before Kiri and I were in the clear; get on The Queen without Madam Aveline catching wind of it. We'd already been gone all night, so she was surely on alert.

We dismounted near the docks, where a large rowboat waited for us. Finn turned to me as Lottie and Eric loaded Ben's stuff into the boat.

"Ye come with me," he said.

"To where?"

"To find someone to come and collect the horses and get a few things before we sail." He grabbed a random wooden wagon that looked like it'd seen better days. Probably a communal tool. He tipped his red-bearded chin at Kiri. "And ye need to get supplies for the kitchen, lass."

She beamed up at Ben and looped her arm through his. "Would you come to help me? I'm unsure I could lift a sack of flour or grain myself."

I turned from them all with an eye roll. If only Kiri knew how hard it was for me to resist Ben alone. I didn't need her help in thrusting us together.

"Eric and I will secure a few barrels of fresh water," Lottie chimed in. "Meet back in an hour. Then we row out."

I stuck close to Finn as Ben and Kiri purchased things for the kitchen—sacks of grain and flour, herbs and spices, molasses, dried meats, and butter—always a few merchant tents away. But Ben was always looking at me every time I dared to glance in their direction.

Finn made arrangements with some guy who smelled like a horse, and I just stood by idly as he explained how to get to Ben's farm. The market was bustling with people, buyers and vendors, thieves and barters, beggars, and all sorts of walks of life. Even a couple of girls from the brothel were there, cooing and fawning at men who passed them by, getting sneers from women.

My heart froze.

There were people here from Mademoiselle Aveline's brothel. I whipped my head around, searching for the French woman's dark kohl eyes and notable hairdo, but there were just so many people. I pushed through the sea of bodies in a panic.

"Kiri!" I called and ran when I found Ben. He was alone. I grabbed his arm, eyes wide, and his smile faded as he saw the fear on my face. "Where's Kiri?"

He spun around, confused. "She was here just a moment ago. I turned my back for a moment to grab more flour–"

"Shit!" I pushed back through the crowd, scanning for her fiery hair. "Kiri!"

Behind me, I heard Ben hastily tell the vendor to watch his wagon. He jogged to my side. "What's wrong?"

My heart raced painfully in my chest. "Kiri, I kind of *stole* her from the brothel and Aveleine's goons are here."

Finn appeared. "What's got ye in a tizzy?"

I ran my hands through my hair as I spun back and forth. She was gone. Aveline must have had someone scoop her up quietly and drag her away. "Kiri technically belongs to Madam Aveline, but I was trying to smuggle her off the island so she could find her brother and get home."

Finn put his hands on his hips and released a deep,

growly sigh. "Aye, lass, why am I not surprised? Yer just like–"

I whipped my head around and faced him, my eyes flashing a warning to watch his words. I knew what he meant. Saving a sixteen-year-old girl from a life of sex slavery probably sounded like something my mother would do.

I grabbed hold of both their sleeves. "Come on, we have to get her back."

"Whoa, whoa!" Ben said, skidding to a halt in the dirt. "We can't just march in there and take one of her girls, Ace. She's got hired muscle in every corner, and the woman's decked with knives and guns herself beneath all those layers of skirts."

"I promised I would help her!"

Finn leaned in, holding me by both arms, his voice calm. "And ye will, lass. I swear it. But we need a plan."

I couldn't form a straight thought. My mind swirled with panic. Would Aveline punish Kiri for trying to leave? Would she kill her? I didn't have time to wait and make plans or get the rest of the crew. Part of me doubted Lottie would even help, anyway.

Finn's pistol gleamed in the sun as his jacket flapped open, and I didn't give it a second thought. I grabbed the gun and took off running. Behind me, I could hear them both grumble, but two pairs of boots only took half a second to sound thudding in the dirt.

I ran to the brothel and slipped around back where I knew Kiri's bedroom window balcony was. I craned my neck upward, sizing up just how out-of-reach it was. The second story…there was no way–but a lower window had a sturdy-looking awning over it. If I stood on it, I could manage to reach the sill.

Ben and Finn skidded to a stop, and without missing a beat, Finn bent his knees, his hands braided together, ready to hoist me up. I grabbed his shoulders and placed my boot in his waiting hands. The beastly Scot vaulted me into the air, and I climbed onto the awning as quietly as possible, which wasn't quiet at all. I'd have to move fast.

I stretched and climbed Kiri's wrought iron balcony and prayed she was in her room. I assumed Aveline had locked her in there. The sheer linens in the window billowed in the breeze, swatting me in the face. I pushed them aside and peered into the room. She sat crying on her bed, and my heart sank.

Making sure she was alone, I made a *psst* sound to catch her attention. She glanced around, eyes puffy and red, but her whole face brightened at seeing me.

"Come on," I whispered, waving her to the balcony.

Kiri jumped up and slammed into my arms, crushing me into a hug. "You came for me."

I shushed her, my heart racing. "Of course. I promised

I'd get you off this island." I glanced down below where Ben and Finn waited. "We have to climb down, okay?" She looked at me, panicked and doubtful. "You can do this. I climbed up here. It's not as far as it looks. And they'll catch you."

Kiri shook her head as she examined the two-story drop. I took her sweet, freckled face in my hands. "Look at me, Kiri, look at me. You can do this. We need to move fast. Aveline could come any moment."

"Okay," she replied and held my hands with trembling ones.

I eased her over the railing as she slid down the spindles and hung from the bottom of the balcony.

"We've got you, Kiri," Ben said just loud enough for her to hear. Finn mirrored him and held out his arms. She let go with a quiet yelp, and their arms softened her landing.

The bedroom door swung open, and Aveline and two men stormed in. One cocked a gun at me, and I turned and bolted for the window. I didn't have time to carefully climb over the railing, so I flung myself over it as hard as I could, my muscles remembering how I used to fly about the bars in gymnastics, and I narrowly landed on the awning below. The wooden canopy splintered and burst as I crashed to the ground. My lungs heaved as the wind knocked from them.

I struggled to breathe as my three friends dove to

help me.

"My, Benjamin," Aveline cooed from up on the balcony. She fanned herself with a little black lace fan. "How we've missed you here. Why don't you visit anymore?"

Air slowly settled in my lungs again. But Ben looked sick. Kiri helped me to my feet, and I threw Aveline a middle finger. "Maybe he realized he was better than the trash you keep."

I saw his head turn to me from the corner of my eye.

"Your lease on the girl is over," Aveline replied, crossing her bony arms. "For trying to steal her."

My ankle throbbed with just a bit of weight, but I threw her a narrowed look. "Fine by me. But she's still coming with me."

She just stood there, almost…smugly. The sound of quick footsteps sounded, and we tensed as we looked around. Her two henchmen came running toward us, one with a pistol, one with a sword.

"We need to go!" Ben said, shoving us along.

We ran off, but my bum ankle slowed me down, and I fell to the back. I managed to keep up, though, and I knew we only had a short distance to the docks. We just had to get to the rowboat.

A gunshot pierced the air, and something cut the air right next to my ear. A bullet. Suddenly, my ankle didn't hurt as much, and adrenaline, mixed with fear, pushed me further, faster. Another few gunshots sent more whizzing sounds, just a hair's breadth from my face. I ducked and darted out of the way, covering my head.

Half turned and still running, Finn reached an arm back. "Gimmie my pistol, lass!" I shoved the gun I stole from him in his hand. He cocked it and fired a single shot that hit one guy right between the eyes. He cocked it again and then grumbled. "Empty!"

But we were at the boat in a few moments.

The other man had stopped over his friend's corpse, buying a few seconds for us to climb inside the wooden boat. I shoved Kiri down to the floor and covered her. Ben readied the oars and began rowing us away from the dock as Finn packed his gun again with lead balls.

But Aveline's henchman was there, toes over the edge as he fired his gun at us. Kiri screamed beneath me, and I turned my head enough to steal a peek up at Ben, who moved the oars, grunting and groaning with every row. More bullets fired, some from the dock, some from Finn. The lead balls pelted by, making dents in the wood and splashing in the water.

Ben glanced down at me, and our eyes locked for a split second. His shoulder cocked back, and he keeled over in pain, struggling to hold the oars as they flopped about. I grabbed one just as it nearly slipped from the doe pin.

"Damn it! Finn!" he shouted, hand clamped over his

shoulder. "Take the oars!"

My pulse shot through the roof when I realized what had happened. Blood oozed between Ben's fingers as he clasped a hand over a bullet wound in his upper arm. He and Finn clumsily traded places, climbing over Kiri and me on the boat floor, and he took the heavy oars.

"Stay down, lass!"

Finn bolted us through the water toward The Queen, and Ben tried to hide his massive frame as low as possible while tearing a strip of fabric from the hem of his shirt. I watched in pure shock as he poorly wrapped the wound, moaning in pain as he tightened it.

Bullets continued to fire but barely reached the boat, so I knew it was just a matter of moments before we were finally out of range. But a lead ball hit the side of the boat just a hair from my head, and a rush of anger pissed through me. I shot to my knees, grabbed Finn's gun again, outstretched my arm toward the dock, and fired. It took two shots, but I nicked the guy in the leg, and he hit the ground.

Ben laughed in disbelief, and I turned to Finn, handing him the pistol back. "Sorry."

He chuckled, sweat beading down his forehead. "Dinnae be sorry, lass. But we may need to get a pistol fer ye."

I shakily stood up and climbed over the seat that protected Kiri, my attention on Ben. "Are you—"

A blinding pain exploded in my shoulder, knocking me back. I stumbled, unable to catch my footing, and the last thing I saw as I tumbled over the side of the boat was Ben reaching over the seat, eyes wide with fear, and the gunman behind him in the distance, lying across the dock with his pistol still pointed at me.

And then my body hit the water.

CHAPTER ELEVEN

The ocean grabbed me and carried my bleeding body through a strange undertow. My head already swirled from lack of oxygen…and blood. My shoulder left a deep red trail in the water as something dragged me along.

Hands appeared on my waist, and a siren appeared, her whole ethereal body writhing and moving as she cut through the sea with me in her grasp.

But…it wasn't a siren; it was something else. A beautiful creature with a human look behind its eyes—large black almond-shaped eyes. *A mermaid.* The word popped into my mind like a fuzzy memory. Mom mentioned in her journal a sea beast, unlike a siren, that blew into her mouth just before she washed ashore on Ben's cursed island.

The mermaid stopped, and we were suspended as she examined my bullet wound. Blood still sifted from it, and my lungs burned. She cupped her mouth over mine, and I welcomed the air that inflated my chest.

You do not need that.

I gasped and took a mouthful of water. She seemed to sigh and blew more air into me, forcing the salt water out.

I don't know how to use any of my siren abilities, I thought, hoping that was how it worked.

She tilted her head and rubbed her long fingers over my bullet hole. A strange silver light connected her hand and the wound, and a twinge of pressure bloomed in my shoulder as she extracted the lead ball.

She pinched it between her thumb and finger, examining it closely with a cat-like curiosity. She curled her fingers around it and smiled at me with a toothy grin.

I could already feel the flesh stitching itself back together. What kind of magic was this?

You must stay away from Benjamin Cook, she warned. *You cannot risk slipping up and messing with the future.*

What would happen?

She shook her head. *No one knows how time truly works.*

And anyone who says they do is a liar. But if Benjamin Cook were to find out who you are and how you came to be here, there's no telling what effect that could have on the timeline, if any.

A shadow moved in the water behind her. Someone was swimming toward me.

It was Ben.

The mermaid tensed and gave me one last look. *Don't risk it.* And she bolted away.

Whatever hold the mermaid had on me that had kept me suspended broke away, and I flailed in the water. But Ben was there, one massive arm wrapped around my waist, the other swimming us back to the surface. His muscled legs kicked, and I did the same, hoping it would get us there faster.

We broke the surface just feet from The Queen, and I gasped for air, the breath gurgling in my mouth as sea-water spat from my throat. He kept one arm tightly hooked around me.

"Are you okay?" he asked, exasperated.

"I'm fine. It just nicked me," I lied. "I…tripped." Blood had already soaked through his makeshift bandage. "What about you?"

Ben seemed unsure, and I turned in the water, hiding my shoulder from him. "I've had worse," he said, wading us toward the rope netting hanging from the ship's side.

He helped me climb onto it, a curious and worried look

on his face as he noted the way I grasped the rope with ease. He momentarily waited for me to gain a few feet, then began climbing behind me.

"I saw…I could have sworn the bullet hit you."

Even fully healed, my slender arms burned with strain, and I made a mental note that if I found a way home, I'd start going to the gym. We reached the top, and Ben helped me over the wooden railing. We rolled to the floor, panting, wet, and utterly exhausted.

"Let me see," he said, rolling over and reaching for my jacket.

He glimpsed the bullet hole, and I found the strength to hop to my feet. "I said I'm fine."

Lottie and the rest of the crew, minus a night-dwelling Cynda, were there. The mermaid's words of caution rang in my ears. Letting myself get too close to Ben could lead to unfortunate results. Who knew how my presence had already impacted the future I once knew.

I looked at Lottie, fresh breath still burning down my throat and lungs. "So, where to first, Captain?"

CHAPTER TWELVE

After a quick stop at a neighboring island to stock up on the things we accidentally left behind in the market, The Queen pushed out to sea, and a week flew by as we all settled into our roles. Kiri in the kitchen, me on the deck. Finn divided his time between the helm, helping me navigate all the ropes, gear, and moving parts I was tasked with using.

Eric helped out occasionally where he could, but he spent most of his time in the captain's quarters with Lottie, pouring over maps and scrolls. Sometimes I'd glanced up and catch her watching me with a dead look, and I wondered what she was thinking. Was Finn right? Did Lottie really know who I was but refused to admit it?

Cynda spent the daylight hours below deck; she occupied the belly of the ship but came up during the evenings to give me and Ben relief from our duties.

Ben only took a few days to get the hint that I was avoiding him. I didn't stay long in any spaces we shared, I didn't strike up any conversations, and I kept my gaze low as I worked alongside him, only speaking in reply to his questions and comments. Near the end of the first week, he just gave up trying to reconnect with me.

Guilt riddled me, and I knew he must have assumed it was something he'd done. But how could I explain my reasoning for suddenly putting a boundary between us? I couldn't exactly say that I was from the future, here to play a siren's twisted game, and a friendly mermaid warned me to stay away from him.

It was a calm afternoon, and Finn told me to take a break while he watched over the helm. Relief pushed down on me. The Queen was considered a small ship by most standards, but it was still some of the hardest work I'd ever done in my life. My arms and legs throbbed as I headed down the mess deck and to the kitchen, where Kiri was preparing things for supper.

I pushed through the swinging doors and found Eric

and her talking closely, and Kiri let out a stream of giggles that cut short at the sight of me. Eric's face changed back to his stoic mask, and I couldn't help but feel I'd interrupted something.

I grabbed a fresh bun and sat on a stool in the corner. "Don't let me keep you," I told them. "I'm just here to kill some time and take a break from the deck."

Eric cleared his throat and adjusted his pristine jacket, and I failed to hide the scoffing sound that turned over in my throat. I was layered in dirt, sweat, and blood. My only outfit clung to my grimy skin, and here he stood, looking freshly bathed, with hardly a speck of dirt on him. I wondered then if it were magic. He was a sorcerer, after all. I wanted to ask if he could magically clean me up, but that felt like a silly thing to ask. Plus…I had the feeling Eric didn't quite like me for some reason. He hardly spoke a word to me, was quiet in my presence, and always seemed to have this mask that I'd first thought was just his normal face, but soon realized he wore it for me.

"I suppose I should check in with our sailing master," Eric noted with a hint of sarcasm. He smiled at Kiri, and a blush bloomed beneath her unsure expression. He grimaced blankly at me as he passed on the way to the door.

Did he know more than he let on? Did his sorcerer abilities give him some kind of weird insight toward other magical beings? Because, as much as it pained me to admit it, I was a magical being. Siren's blood flowed in my veins, and I was a time traveler, after all.

I looked at Kiri. "What the hell did he want?"

She shrugged and busied about the kitchen, tossing dirty dishes in a tub and wiping down the butcher block. "Nothing, he was just being nice."

My suspicion increased. "I didn't think he was capable of such a thing."

"Oh, please," she replied, tipping her head to the side as she stirred a steaming pot. "Eric's just the quiet type. Talk to him, get to know him."

Something told me no amount of talking would get that guy to crack a smile for me.

"What are you doing here?" she asked. "Aren't you on duty?"

"Finn said I could take a break. The water's calm, so we're just sort of coaxing along." I grabbed another bun and lobbed off a bite. "Need any help?"

Kiri's red waves shook loosely. "No, thank you." She wiped her hands on her apron. "Stew is nearly ready for supper. Buns are cooling." She leaned over and slapped my hand as I reached for a third.

She looked so at home in the kitchen aboard a pirate ship full of people I wasn't even sure we could trust. "Don't get too comfortable," I warned her just above a whisper. "I'm getting you on a ship back home as soon as possible."

"Perhaps…" She thought for a moment. "Perhaps I don't need to go home."

"What about your brother?"

"He's not there. No one is," Kiri replied. "My village was burnt to the ground. Anyone who escaped the raiders is surely long gone. There's…there's nothing for me to return to."

"But you can't give up on finding your brother, Kiri. He's out here somewhere, probably looking for you."

"And I'm not giving up my search for him, either," she said, but I could hear the uncertainty in her voice. "But maybe I could do it with the help of people who don't want to use me, that don't see me as nothing more than my virtue."

This was Eric's doing. He'd been filling her head with ideas of joining their pirate crew. Or maybe there was some other motive for him weaseling in and around her. But I didn't want to jump to conclusions yet and alarm her.

"Just…be careful, Kiri."

I stood from the stool and quickly grabbed another bun, ignored the wooden spoon she swatted in my direction, and left. I'd been dancing around the idea of Eric not being trustworthy for over a week now. Maybe it was time he and I had a chat. I pretended to meander about the ship, making small talk with Finn, a quick head nod exchanged with Lottie through the window of her quarters, and noted how Eric was nowhere to be seen.

The deck was quiet as I strolled about, staring out over the never-ending ocean. The sight would have reduced me to a bundle of nerves just a few weeks ago. Growing up a stone's throw from the sea when it terrified you to your core was a burden I'd kept to myself, even from my family.

I'd filled my time with extracurricular activities stacked on top of one another; dance, karate, and rock climbing were some of my favorites. But I loved playing and my grandmother's swords on her back deck as she instructed me to hold, wield, and use them. Standing on the deck of The Queen, a ship my parents once sailed, I couldn't help but wonder if I'd somehow been preparing myself. In these circumstances, I possessed everything I needed to survive in this time. And maybe the siren knew that.

It was time I started playing the game. I had to figure out how my parent's old friends could help me get home. Having Finn in the know was a bonus, but I'd yet to figure out my next move. But, one detail nagged at me; there was a sorcerer aboard the ship, and if I learned anything from my parent's story, it was that magic users could help create relics that could send you through time. My mother had an enchanted snow globe, and they'd once used my nan's ring to get home. Maybe if I talked to Eric and got to know him, he could help.

I just had to figure out how to do that without revealing who I really was.

I went below deck, past the mess hall, past the sleeping quarters where we stayed, searching for the stoic sorcerer. But he was nowhere to be found. I went deeper into the belly of the ship, where shadows stretched from side to side and portholes were nothing but glass views into the sea. The stench of musk and mold filled my nose and made my eyes water.

A labored moan sifted through the air, and I followed the sound. As I neared, I could tell it was a man's groans of pain and exhaustion, but another voice mixed with it.

Cynda.

She stood over a naked man, and he peered up at her with a strange look. His wrists were bound and chained, his bruised and dirty body hanging from the chains. She paced before him like a lion about to pounce on its kill, but he stared back with delight.

I watched, frozen in horror, from behind a stack of water barrels as she lifted his arm to her nose and inhaled deeply before sinking her teeth into his flesh. Bile rose from my stomach, and I clamped a hand over my mouth to keep from screaming, but I couldn't look away. The man was clearly in pain, and Cynda kept him chained up to torture. But…he seemed to enjoy it. She drank from his forearm as his other hand rattled the chains, reaching down to start pleasuring himself.

A gasp escaped from me, and Cynda's back stiffened. Silence fell over the room, and I knew I had to go, but my feet were lead as she slowly spun around, eyes black as night with dark veins crawling outward like spiderwebs.

She was across the room in a split second and had me by the neck. "What are you doing down here?"

I strained to speak as she squeezed my throat. "I-I was looking for Eric."

"He knows better than to venture this deep." Those monstrous black eyes flashed with delight. "As should you." Her clawed fingers dug into my flesh, threatening to puncture it, and a whimper erupted from me. She leaned in, dragging her nose up and down the throbbing veins on my neck. "Ahh, I knew there was something about you."

I carefully reached for the dagger at my side and wrapped my fingers around the hilt. In one swift movement, I thrust the tip into her stomach, and she released me. Choking on the influx of air, I bolted in the opposite direction, trying to remember how far the nearest ladder hatch was. Behind me, Cynda's footsteps sounded faster than my racing heart, and I pumped my arms, willing myself to move faster.

I slammed into a ladder, nearly knocking it over, and scrambled up the steps as she clawed at my feet. I wasted no time on the next level and took off running again, but she was hot on my heels. Ahead, I spotted a beam of sunlight coming in through a porthole, and I dove for it just as Cynda's arms reached for me. The sunlight touched her skin, instantly searing it, and she backed away with a hiss.

"You're insane!" I screamed through labored breaths.

She chuckled evilly as she continued backing away. "You have no idea."

I waited until the shadows engulfed her and made sure she was gone before I ran to the next ladder hatch, only stopping in the streaks of sunshine that cut through the dank air to glance over my shoulder.

I was on a ship with monsters and sailed on a sea of them.

CHAPTER THIRTEEN

BEN

Ace's scream sent my blood searing. I dropped the bundle of rope I'd been coiling and took off toward the echo of her voice. My feet barely touched the steps as I slid down the ladder to the mess deck, my eyes frantically searching for her head of white curls. Did she cut herself with a knife? Burn herself with boiling water?

No, her scream was guttural.

I ran and ran until I heard footsteps barreling toward me so fast that I hardly had time to stop as she slammed into me. She was frantic, terrified, her hands trembling. Those charcoal eyes stared at me, full of fright, and I held her close.

"Shhh, it's okay, it's okay," I said.

"She's a *monster!*"

One arm firm at her back, I held her face in my palm and willed her to calm down. I could feel the terror that wreaked havoc inside her. She kept looking over her shoulder.

"Ace, what happened?"

Her fingers grappled with my shirt as if searching for something to hold onto. "Cynda, she–her eyes–the man–"

"Breathe," I said firmly and proceeded to show her a deep inhale and exhale. Finally, her eyes cleared, and she saw me for the first time, her frightened stare locking on mine as she matched her breathing to mine. The shaking subsided, but I refused to let her go. "Okay, now tell me what happened. Are you alright?"

Ace nodded. "I…I was looking for Eric, and I wandered to the lower decks. But Cynda…she has someone tied up. She's *feeding* on him."

It took everything in me not to run down there myself. "Did she hurt you?"

She shook her head. "No, she tried to, though."

I put a hand on her back, leading her in the direction I came. "Come on, let's have a talk with Lottie."

Rage burned through my veins and toiled in my gut, but every step we took toward the upper deck was one step

I wasn't taking toward Cynda. I wanted to kill the bitch. We shouldn't have a creature so untrustworthy aboard our ship. I knew it before we sailed. But Lottie needed her, and I knew better than to come between Charlotte and her plans.

But I wouldn't hesitate to slice her throat if she laid another finger on Ace.

I kept my arm around Ace's shoulders as we walked to the captain's quarters, and I didn't bother knocking. Lottie looked up from her pile of maps and scrolls, brows pinched together in an expression that said, *how dare you.*

"Don't fucking look at me like that!" I bellowed. "You brought that monster on board, and she attacked Ace."

Lottie opened her mouth to reply, but Ace added, "Not to mention, she has a *human being* chained up down there, and she's *feeding* on him."

She turned her attention to a stack of papers in her hand. "I don't concern myself with Cynda's activities."

"Wait," Ace replied, shocked. "You *knew?*"

Lottie tossed the papers on the desk and gave her a bored look of impatience. "Cynda is imperative to the mission, and she has special needs, so I look the other way."

How far the lovely had fallen. This wasn't the loyal and brave woman I once knew.

Ace guffawed. "I can't believe this! I can *not* believe you'd ever allow something like that to happen on *your* watch."

Lottie's blue eyes flashed with a challenge. "And who the hell are you to presume *anything* about me?"

The two engaged in a stare-down, the tension solidifying between them. I couldn't help but feel there was something else afoot here.

I stepped into the space between them. "She may not know you, Charlotte, but I do. This isn't you; this isn't what we stand for, and you know it."

She set her viper look on me, rimmed with exhaustion. God, was she even sleeping?

"What, you think because I let you in my bed a few times that you *know* me? You know nothing about me!" A knife appeared in her hand, and she spun it through her fingers with expert skill before spiking it into her desk. "*Nothing!*"

From the corner of my eye, I saw Ace stifle a gasp and take a step back. I just shook my head at Lottie. We'd sworn to never speak of those times, to forget all about our moments of loneliness. To throw it in my face now, in front of someone…

It was spite and maybe a little jealousy that fueled her actions. I could see it in her eyes. Charlotte and I had no romantic connection, but she was a territorial kind of woman, and something about Ace picked at her. I just couldn't figure out what. The Lottie I once knew would have been happy that I'd found someone that interested me, someone who seemed to care for me in a way I deserved.

I shook my head, disappointed, and stormed out of the room. It only took half a second for Ace to follow, but I didn't stop. I strode across the deck, headed for the ladder hatch, but her hand grabbed at my shoulder, forcing me to turn around.

I wasn't prepared for the look of betrayal in her glistening eyes.

"Is it true?" she asked. "Did you…sleep with her?"

Why was she upset? Although my budding feelings grew with every moment I spent in her presence, we barely knew one another. Did this woman care for me deeper than I realized? Was I slipping into my same old routine?

"It was a long time ago, purely out of loneliness," I admitted with a shrug.

She nodded, pressing her lips together. "I see." She wavered for a moment, then motioned behind her. "I'm…I have to go see if Kiri needs help in the kitchen."

I stood there, bewildered as I watched her leave, suddenly worried I'd destroyed something before it began. But was I mistaken? Perhaps I was reading her wrong.

No, I knew a hurting heart when I saw one. Mine had ached for years.

CHAPTER FOURTEEN

AUDREY

After learning of Ben and Lottie's past and nearly becoming a vampire's next meal, I couldn't bring myself to go below decks. So, I spent the rest of the day on the quarter deck, staring out at the trail we left behind in the sea as a dark navy sky slowly fell over the ship, and a silver moon replaced the sun above.

Word must have spread about what happened below decks because no one bothered me. Nobody came to say I had duties or a job to do. It was the most peaceful moment I'd had since washing up ashore in the past. Peaceful…yet I was riddled with foreign emotions. I'd never cared for a man like I did for Ben, and *this* Ben…he wasn't mine.

He wasn't the man I fell in love with and was ripped away from.

Finn was the first to come to find me. "Aye, lass," he said, sidling up to me as we stared at the sea together. "Ye goin' to stay up here all day?"

I glanced around us to make sure no one was listening. "Did…did my mom have a hard time, too? At first?"

He tipped his head back. "That she did. I remember the first moment I spotted her, a heap of black curls soaking in the water, draped over a wooden chest. We thought she was dead."

"How did she cope?" I asked. "How did she deal with being inserted in three hundred years in the past?"

"Yer ma never told you stories?"

"She did, both her and Dad," I replied. "Plenty, but they were all tales of your adventures. The only hardships I know of are the ones I read about in her journals. But they're cherry-picked." He scrunched his brows together. "Uh, selective. She chose to only share certain things."

"Aye, well, I can assure ye that yer ma struggled," he told me. "In the beginning and right to the end. It was why she chose to go back, to raise ye wee things in the future where it was safe."

The staircase creaked beneath Kiri's gentle footsteps, and I turned to find her walking toward me with a steaming bowl. Finn gave me a quick nod that said we could resume this conversation later and passed Kiri as he descended the stairs.

She smiled and handed me a bowl. "You didn't come to supper," she said. "I worked hard on that stew, you know."

My dry lips pulled at the edges as I smiled back and inhaled the heady aroma wafting from the bowl. "Thanks," I said and patted a crate next to me. "I just needed some time to clear my head."

She sat down. "I heard about what happened."

I shoved spoonful after spoonful of meat and potatoes into my mouth. I hadn't realized how starved I was.

"Everyone was quiet at supper," she continued. "So, I told them they should all be ashamed of themselves for ignoring what happened."

"Kiri!"

She lifted her chin and straightened her back. "What? It's true. We're all part of a crew here. If one of us attacks another, it *should* be addressed."

"I did address it," I grumbled.

"Yes, and you were dismissed as if it were nothing."

Lottie called out over the deck from her doorway, summoning everyone to gather around. I stood, my back protesting from sitting for so many hours, and followed Finn to the short railing looking down over the rest of the crew.

Eric stood next to Finn with a mop in hand, a displeased look on his face at having to perform duties that weren't his. Clearly, Finn had made him pick up the slack in my absence. With the sun gone, Cynda appeared from a ladder hatch, her pale skin gleaming in the moonlight. Dark leather hugged her lithe body, and her black curls were pinned back neatly.

She was undoubtedly a creature of the night; she was practically made of it. Her cat-like stare lifted to where I stood, an unreadable look on her face. I swallowed nervously but just stared back at her with indifference. I would not show weakness.

Lottie juggled a set of dice in her hand. "Tensions are high. So, there's only one way to dissolve it."

Finn's mouth formed into a delighted grin, and he rubbed his hands together. "Poker!"

Kiri and I exchanged a look of disbelief. Really? This was how she wanted to address the fact that her hired monster tried to kill me? With a card game?

Next to Finn, Ben peered up at me with a warm look of concern and hope. "What do you say, Ace?"

Eric gave a miffed sound as he crossed his arms. "The girls probably never played an honest game of cards in their lives."

I was about to retort, but Kiri gripped the railing. "I'll have you know, sir, I cleaned out many a man and sent them walking with empty pockets."

I wasn't too bad at poker, either. So, I grinned confidently, standing next to my friend, and nodded to the rest of them. "Bring it on."

We gathered on the mess deck and surrounded the rectangle table. Finn had grabbed a few jars of rum while Lottie dealt the cards. Kiri fetched a bowl of buns and a plate of jerky and set it in the center of the table as Finn popped the top off one of the jars and took a big swig before handing it to me.

I wiped the top and poured a mouthful down my throat. It was a welcome burn, and I let out a rough sigh as I handed it to Lottie. We all took our cards in hand as the bottle circulated around the table, from Lottie to Cynda, Eric, Ben, Kiri, and Finn again.

Lottie held her hand close and peered over her cards at everyone. "Alright, you know the game. Twos are wild. Let's play."

I watched intently as, one by one, items were added to the center of the table amongst the bowls of food. Coins, gems, stones, jewelry. The rum made its way back to me, and I took the opportunity to pause and consider what I had. I reached into my pocket and pulled out a few loose coins. Two gold and three silver. I tossed them on the pile.

We played two fairly quiet rounds—Lottie won both—but the jar of rum kept making its rounds, and the conversation began to strike up. Halfway through our game, tensions melted away, and, for a moment, I could forget all about the shitty situation I was stuck in because I was sitting at a table, eating good food, drinking strong rum with a bunch of treasure hunters.

And I had a really good hand.

"Anti-up," Finn said and cackled to himself as he tossed in a handful of coins with a purposeful grin. He was a dead giveaway.

Everyone else added to the pile, and I gloated inside. I had a *really* good hand. I dug around in my pocket for my little bag of goodies, picked out the other ruby from my earrings, and placed it on top of a stack of gold coins.

Five looks of surprise pointed at me, but Kiri just smiled, knowing of my teensy fortune.

"Alright," Lottie said, glancing around at our circle. "Show 'em."

We all laid our hands down, one by one. Finn grumbled loudly and slapped his crappy cards down in front of him. There were some good hands, but I had a flush. My arms shot in the air, ready to cheer myself on, but Kiri then laid down a royal flush, and everyone erupted in cheer and laughter.

Finn clapped her on the back, nearly knocking her forward. "Good fer ye, lass!"

Her soft cheeks flushed red as she smiled proudly and scooped her winnings toward her chest. She glanced up at me.

I just laughed. "I didn't know you were a shark."

Everyone paused and looked at me strangely. Shark, poker shark. That wasn't a term in this time. I scrambled through my thoughts.

"Poker shark. I think…it means hiding your hand well." I swallowed nervously. "I, uh, overheard some men using it at the brothel."

Most of the crew shrugged it off and began collecting the cards to be dealt again, but Finn and Lottie exchanged a look. She had to have known who I was. I cleared my throat and moistened it with another generous gulp of warm beer.

"So," Ben piped up and turned toward Eric. "What's your story?"

Eric held that same unbothered look of contempt he always had. "No story to speak of."

"Ahh, come on," Ben replied. "We've all got a story. How did you meet Lottie?"

"I joined her crew after being lost in Jamestown."

A man of few words and details. What was he hiding?

Cynda leaned forward; with her leather corset removed, her white blouse hung open, revealing more of that pale, otherworldly skin.

"Lost?" she balked. "We pulled his sorry ass from a burning ship in the harbor. I heard his cries from the shore and swam out while Lottie followed behind in a rowboat."

Lottie spoke as she dealt the cards. "He was so badly burned, I thought he would die. But then he used magic to heal himself, and I knew he had to be on my crew."

Ben chortled as he picked up his cards. "Still collecting people, Charlotte?"

She glared at him. "Collecting, saving, giving purpose. Call it what you will, *Benjamin*."

A strange silence fell over us once again as we collected our hands and sifted through the cards. Across the table, I caught Cynda's glance, and she gave me a genuine smile.

"I would like to apologize for my…behavior earlier," she told me. "I have little control when I'm feeding, but I assure you it won't happen again." Finn stifled a sarcastic sound, and she cut a look at him. "As long as you stay away from the lower decks."

Ben pressed his lips together, an unreadable look on his face. "What about that man you have tied up down there?"

A devilish look glazed over her eyes. "The conditions are his by choice. The man has a…penchant for pain which suits my needs just fine."

A shiver crept down my spine.

"Have you truly never heard of vampires before?" Eric asked. I wondered if anyone else could sense the different tone he always used with me. Like it was heavier, harder for him to even talk to me.

"Well, yes, I've *heard* of them," I replied. *In fiction.* "And with the other creatures roaming about, I guess it shouldn't be a surprise."

Cynda's long fingers splayed her cards in front of her. "And what other creatures do you mean?"

I shrugged and cast a look at Lottie. "Well, I know we're about to attempt caging a kraken. And I've…heard, uh, stories about sirens."

Lottie sneered to herself. "Fucking beasts. Those scourges should be eradicated. Every last one of them and their wretched wish pearls."

Ben shifted uncomfortably.

"And you?" I asked him. "What's your stance on sirens?"

"I hate them," he replied calmly, but his eyes spoke much more.

I chewed at the inside of my cheek, unsure whether to ask the question that plagued me. But if anyone knew the information I needed, they'd surely be at this table.

"What…what about blood pearls?"

I was met with mostly curious looks, but Cynda froze and stared right at me. "What do you know of blood pearls, girl?"

I shrugged, playing it cool. "Just stories, myths. I wondered what they did, if–if they were like wish pearls."

She chortled and leaned back. "Surely not–"

A noise from above sent us all on alert. Finn and Lottie jumped to their feet, hands on their weapons. Ben was at my side immediately, arm at my back, and I pressed against him without a thought. We just…gravitated toward one another.

"What's happening," I whispered.

He tensed against me. "Someone's on the ship."

My heart kicked into gear, and panic seared my veins. Pirates raiding *pirates*? Or were they treasure hunters now? Ben's mouth was in my hair, whispering in my ear. "Go. Take Kiri and slip into one of the quarters below. Lock the doors."

I turned from him. "Absolutely not. I can help. I can fight." I only had my parent's dagger strapped to my thigh. "Just give me a weapon."

Ben seemed about to argue otherwise, but Lottie handed me a pistol. "You've got a good shot," she said.

I nodded thanks and took the gun, stuffing it in the back of my pants beneath my jacket. If only she knew I was better with a sword than a pistol. My father used to take me hunting a few times a year. But my grandmother taught me everything she knew about swords.

I turned to Kiri. "Go downstairs and hide in your room. Lock the door. Put things up against it."

She looked at me with brave doe eyes. "I can help."

"Yes, by not being something we have to worry about."

I gently shoved at her. "Go, now, before it's too late."

With just a moment's pause, she took off and silently disappeared.

Lottie led the way, and we dispersed to different sides of the ship. Ben and I to the left, Finn to the right, Eric and Lottie above the captain's quarters, looking down over our guests. All thirteen of them.

A small mob of men and a fuck load of weapons.

"Shit," I whispered to myself, and Ben's chest vibrated with a low growl as he stared them down.

"Gentlemen," Lottie called out, her navy jacket blowing open in the breeze. "To what do I owe the pleasure of your visit?"

One of the men, front and center, sneered up at her with a murderous grin. "We hear there's a ship in the area that carries a king's treasure."

"And you're here to steal, I presume?"

He made a mocking bow, and his crew began to laugh. Guns cocked all around, swords unsheathed, and Lottie gave one look to her right and left flanks with a single nod. *Get ready.*

She flung the flaps of her coat back, revealing a dozen knives strapped to her waist and thighs. "It's actually a duke's treasure, but it's still quite impressive." She expertly flicked around a sharp knife in each hand, a hungry look on her face. "But you won't be getting it, either way."

She flung both blades toward the men so fast they were just flicks of light in the moonlight, and they lodged in the pirate's chest next to their leader. He fell to the deck with a heavy thud. A brief assessing pause fell over everyone, and I could hear my heart pounding in my ears.

"Stay close to me," Ben said as the wall of pirates charged at us.

Lottie and Eric rushed down the stairs to the right, joining Finn, and Ben and I took a left. Bullets fired, narrowly zinging by my ears, swords swung, and cries of pain shot across the deck. Ben never left my side, acting as my human shield while he kept one arm pointed outward, firing off lead balls and only breaking to reload. When he did, I lifted my pistol to shield him, dagger firmly gripped at my side.

Finn hacked through a circle of raiders with his broadsword while Lottie flung a stream of never-ending knives, and Eric skirted the crowd, eyeing both sides and only using his magic as a defense when a rogue pirate charged at him. Perhaps he was like me, scared, unsure, and completely inexperienced in combat, but he hid it with a permanent look of disdain.

The raiders still outnumbered us, but we were gaining on them. My bullets never landed a kill shot, but I brought several of them to their knees with bleeding shins, ready to be finished by the others. Someone grabbed my arm, pulling me from Ben, and my gun fell to the floor. I screamed as I tried to yank free, the socket at my shoulder protesting as I did.

"Ace!" Ben called as three pirates held him back. He broke one arm free and punched a guy in the face. I could hear the crack of his nose over all the noise.

My capturer also grappled with freeing me of my dagger, but I refused to let go. We both gripped the handle and when his palms slipped over the hilt, closer to the blade, I gave one mighty tug and sliced through the flesh of his hands.

"Stupid bitch!" he spat as he backed away, nursing his bleeding hands. His heel kicked my gun, and he grinned madly as he bent down to fetch it.

I backed away, not realizing I only had a stack of wooden crates behind me until I nearly stumbled backward over them. He cocked my pistol and pointed it at me, blood dripping down.

I closed my eyes as he shoved the tip into my temple. "It's a pity," he breathed warmly in my face, nearly making me gag. "We could have used you aboard our ship."

Something shot from the sky, landing on him, and all the air huffed from his lungs as Cynda kneeled on his chest. She grabbed him by the neck and looked at me darkly over her shoulder.

"I suggest you get away from me," she said.

I shakily bent down to fetch my gun and nodded as she sunk her teeth into the guy's throat, and I ran in search of Ben, the sound of flesh ripping and a gurgling scream following me. I tried to ignore it as I frantically looked for him and found his massive frame fighting off the same three guys that had pulled him away from me.

I cocked my gun, hoping there were still bullets in it, and fired at one of the pirates. He fell to the deck, and Ben gave me an impressed look as he punched another so hard his head lulled to the side, and his body crumpled to the floor like a ragdoll. The remaining raider had the good sense to run away, but Ben grabbed my gun and shot across the deck, clocking the guy in the back of the head.

Surely, all this death would catch up with me eventually, and I'd fall into a traumatized state, but right now, the rush of the fight, the searing desire to protect myself and my friends…it was exhilarating.

Bodies littered the deck, and I counted our crew, my heart settling down a notch when I noted we were all still standing. Six of us stood around, leaning against barrels or the railing as breath heaved from our lungs.

I looked across at Cynda, whose eyes had returned to normal, but blood dripped down over her chin. "Thank you," I told her, my hands shaking under my crossed arms. "We could have used you the whole time."

Lottie stepped between us, wiping blood from her

blades and returning them to their places on her body. "Cynda serves a few purposes on my crew. One is to dive to the depths of Solomon's grave; the other is offensive scouting."

Cynda nodded dutifully. "I disarmed their cannons and took out the remaining crew."

Oh, so that's where she'd been.

"Excellent," Lottie replied, and it was only then that I noticed the other ship floating alongside The Queen. "Cynda, dump the bodies. Finn, ready the rowboat."

"Where are we going?" I asked. Ben was at my side again.

Lottie pointed the tip of one of her knives toward the raider's ship. "To do what pirate treasure hunters do best."

Ben's fingers brushed mine. "Are you alright?"

I nodded up at him. "Right now? Yes, I'm fine. Later when I'm lying in bed, and everything comes rushing back to me…probably not so much." I inhaled a jittered sigh. "You? Are you okay?"

He gestured to his unmarred appearance. "Not a scratch."

Finn untied the ropes and began lowering the rowboat as the others waited. "I have to go check on Kiri," I told Ben.

"Do you want me to come with you?"

"No." I smiled. "I'll be right back."

I took the back stairs to the lower decks and turned down the narrow hallway that housed the doors to our quarters but stopped momentarily to catch my breath and calm my rattling nerves. This was how my parents lived for years? My mother went back and forth to the past and fought monsters of man and beast alongside my father. It was hard to picture, especially now, having experienced it myself. Mom was always a quiet woman who filled her time with work. Dad was soft and patient, content with what every day brought him.

I pressed my back against the wall and closed my eyes as my head tipped backward. They'd always told me stories of their adventures, but it'd always been just that…*stories*. It's easier to separate the person from the pirate when you've only ever known them as mommy and daddy. But now, I had a newfound respect for my parents.

One of the bedroom doors creaked open, and I opened my eyes. "Kiri! Are you–"

Someone grabbed the front of my jacket and shirt and hauled me inside the room. But it wasn't Kiri.

The raider slammed the door shut and smacked me across the face. I keeled to the side, and he violently searched my body for weapons. I'd left everything up on deck.

I opened my mouth to scream, but he clapped a dirty, grimy hand over it and shoved me onto the bed.

The stench of sweat and rum coated me like a blanket as the pirate stifled my screams with one hand and tore at my clothes with another, holding me down with the weight of his body. I kicked and flailed beneath him, pushing and punching at his chest.

I would not go down like this. This wasn't how my story went.

I wedged my leg between his and brought my knee up as hard as I could, sending him reeling back with a gross, warm exhale of pain.

I scrambled off the bed and readied my stance. There wasn't a chance in hell I was letting this guy take me down and hurt anyone outside that door. I had been in karate for seven years, for Pete's sake. *Seven.* I could take him.

He rolled from the bed and swung at me, but my palm to his chest sent him flying back a few steps. He charged again, but I drove my hand up into his chin. Still, it wasn't enough. He relentlessly dove for me, knocking my feet together, and grabbed my shoulders as I fell onto him. My arm landed across his throat just as his neck hit the wooden edge of the bed, and my entire weight slammed down over him.

The sickening snapping sound filled the small room and triggered a switch inside me. I didn't have to wait for sleep because the reality of everything I'd just witnessed and done crashed over me, and I scrambled to the corner, clutching my torn shirt as if to hold everything in.

And the room closed in on me.

CHAPTER FIFTEEN

BEN

The silent hallway only raised more concern over the scream I heard. No one else seemed to have heard it, but the faint sound of Ace's pitch reached me on the deck, and something inside me said, *GO*.

I stood at the mouth of the narrow galley, stared at the row of doors leading to a private sleeping quarter, and listened. The silence was deafening. I opened the first door, which was my room. Empty.

"Ace!" I called down the hall.

I stilled my breath and listened until the faintest sound caught my ear. A wince, the tiniest cry of pain, but enough to send my heart into my throat. The second door—Eric's

room—was locked, and I slammed my body into it, splinter-
ing the latch, but the room was empty.

I heard another muffled cry and didn't even bother
checking the lock as I threw myself into the third door. It
burst open, and Ace's tiny body was curled in the corner,
half covered by a chair. A man's body lay limp on the floor,
his neck twisted at an unnatural angle.

I fell to my knees before her and lifted her tear-stained
face. Her eyes were wide with fear, a distant gaze pulling
her far away from here.

"Ace," I said as calmly as I could through breaths that
burned my lungs. My voice seemed to lure her back, and I
swiped a thumb over the skin of her wet cheek. "Hey, Ace,
what happened? Are you hurt?"

Her eyes slipped into focus, and stared up at me with
such torment.

"I…" her voice cracked. "I never…he died…in–in my
hands…"

Oh, shit. I'd been around miscreants, killers, and takers
for so long that I almost forgot that some people didn't
live by the blade and bullet. I'd watched Ace shoot down
several men, but this was clearly the first time she'd taken
a life with her hands.

I wrapped my arms around her and took her into
my lap. She melted into me, resting her head against my
chest, grappling with my shirt as if she thought she might

float away.

"It's okay," I promised her. "It gets better, easier. You... forget over time."

She shifted in my arms and peered up at me with those eyes; God...those eyes, I'd do anything to see the pain wiped away. Her gaze fell to my mouth, followed by her soft, warm lips. Everything in me stiffened, urging me to lean away. But I'd been dreaming of kissing Ace since she showed up on my doorstep.

Her tongue slipped into my mouth, warm and inviting, and I held her close as she moved in my arms, positioning herself, so our chests were pressed together. I cradled the back of her head, devouring every kiss she offered. Her fingers found the hem of my shirt, and those hands slid across my stomach.

Those trembling hands.

I pushed away. "Ace, we shouldn't–"

She pulled me back, desperation in her eyes. "Give me one good reason why not."

"Aside from the dead body right there?" I smiled and smoothed the straggled curls away from her face. "I'd be taking advantage."

"It's not taking advantage if I want it."

I kissed the tip of her nose.

Someone cleared their throat in the hall. Kiri stood in the doorway, arms crossed, face ghostly white as she stared at the dead man on the floor. I struggled to my feet beneath Ace's weight and eased her to stand.

"Kiri," I said with a nervous chuckle. "Are you alright?"

She nodded, still staring at the dead body. "I hid in the chest in my room. Is he..."

"Dead? Yes." I confirmed. "He attacked Ace."

Kiri noticed her friend wavering behind me and ran into the room, wrapping her in a tight embrace. I quietly slipped into the hall to give them some space.

"*I just want to go home*," I heard Ace cry into her friend's shoulder.

My heart sank, and my stomach turned. She didn't belong on a pirate ship, hunting down ancient treasures to resurrect the dead. This woman had a home and probably had a family out there worrying for her. I grabbed the body and hoisted him across my shoulders.

"Uh, just come up on deck when you're ready," I told them and left.

Guilt ate away at my insides as I approached the deck. I'd let her kiss me. When she was at her most vulnerable, I'd *let* her kiss me, and I wanted nothing more than to take her right then and there. Would have if that little voice in the back of my mind didn't whisper that it was wrong.

Ace was trying to get home to her family, and I had a habit of falling in love with the first woman who showed me any attention.

I was a monster.

I reached the deck and inhaled a deep breath of salty sea air. Finn and Cynda dumped the last of the bodies overboard, so I let the body I carried fall to the floor.

"Here's one more from down in the barracks," I said, plunking down on a crate. What a mess. What a colossal fucking mess we've all made of our lives. I'd promised Dianna I'd do something with the gift she gave me, and here I was aboard The Queen, roaming the seas for treasure and finding ways to raise the dead.

Ace and Kiri appeared, a tangible quietness draped over their shoulders. Everything inside of me urged me to take her in my arms and tell her everything would be alright. But I couldn't. That would only deepen this connection I felt for her, one I was certain she felt for me. Ace's mission was to return home to her family, wherever that may be, and I couldn't live with myself if I stood in the way of that.

Plus…I was immortal. What kind of life could I offer her while I stayed this way forever and she grew old and died?

I let her be and looked at Lottie.

"Do we really need to do this?"

Lottie's brow crinkled together. "What do you mean?"

I pointed at the ship in the short distance. "Cynda already took care of the crew. Why do we need to go over there?"

She sauntered toward me. "I'm sorry, but do you not understand what *pirate* means?"

"I thought we were treasure hunters?"

She tilted her head to the side as she examined me. "And we're to hunt treasure aboard that ship." When I shook my head and looked away, she added, "Benjamin. It's a ghost ship. If we don't take whatever's aboard it, someone less deserving will. This is the price they pay for raiding our home."

I stood up, towering over her, but she stared at me spitefully. "This isn't a home. It's a death sentence. And Gus would be turning over in his grave if he knew what you've become."

Her mask faltered for just a split second, and those stormy blues turned glossy. "Well," she said, a slight crack in her voice as she squared her jaw, nothing but malice in her eyes. "It's a good thing he's not in a grave, isn't it?"

***

I watched Ben and Lottie have a heated, passive-aggressive argument off to the side. The rest of the crew pretended not to notice. They readied the rowboat on the opposite side of where they'd dumped the bodies.

Finn and Eric stayed behind with Kiri while I climbed into the boat with Ben, Lottie, and Cynda and rowed silently to the raider ship. It wasn't until we slammed against its side and climbed onto the deck that anyone spoke.

"Take whatever looks of value," Lottie said, shoving a canvas bag at me.

I said nothing and took the bag as I headed for a set of steep stairs that led to the decks below. This ship was way bigger than The Queen, with more rooms to explore, dark corners, and hallways for danger to lurk. But Cynda had made sure to take out the crew.

I checked each private quarter down a long hallway and filled my bag halfway with jewels, gems, coins, and other relics that looked like something that would have been in a museum in the future.

With my back to the open door, I picked around a small trunk in one room, and my heart sank. It was mostly children's clothes. I took stock of the room and saw a doll on the bed. What kind of ship was this?

What did Cynda do…

"Find anything good?" she said from behind me, and I half turned to find her leather-clad body lounging in the doorway like a sly cat.

Those otherworldly eyes flashed at me beneath perfect black brows. God, everything about her was inviting, like some deadly flower.

I stretched to my feet and turned my back to the chest.

Could she sense my quickening pulse? I dangled my bag, smiling shakily. "Good enough."

She sauntered into the room, skirting the perimeter like a predator lining up its prey. My heart burned with panic. "So, got yourself a blood pearl, do you?"

Shit. "I don't know what you're talking about."

She pretended to be interested in the wood paneling. "They're rare, you know. The sirens only use them to cast the most wicked of curses."

I lacked the ability to blink and swallowed nervously. "What kind of curses?"

Cynda glanced at me before setting her attention on her nails. "Oh, an eternity of sadness, a death touch where everyone you touch dies." I shivered at that one. "I've even heard of them cursing mortals with their own blood, making them half beast-half human with nowhere to settle."

A breath winced from me, and she grinned with delight. "There. That's the one." She was inches from me now and stared at me with wonder. "You, girl, are cursed by those beasts, aren't you? Their blood runs in your veins?" She grabbed my arm forcefully and shoved the sleeve up before dragging a sharp nail down my skin over the vein. "I've never tasted another immortal before."

I blinked and yanked my arm away. "And you won't."

Cynda mocked innocence and held up both hands. "Of course."

I gnawed at the inside of my cheek for a moment. "How…do I break the curse? How do I get rid of the pearl?"

"You can't. Blood pearls cannot be traded, stolen, or destroyed. I should know. My father helped the sirens create them."

Just how old *was* she?

"You know," she said with an eerie coo as she neared. "I could help. I could drain the blood from your body."

"And how exactly would that be helping?"

Ben appeared in the doorway, and I sighed with relief, but then a thought occurred to me. Was he listening? Did he hear Cynda talk about the curse? I tried to beg him to take me away with just a look. He wavered momentarily, sizing up the situation in the room, and noted my tensed fists at my sides.

"Lottie says we're closer to Solomon's grave than we thought. We should be there before morning if we leave now," he said, motioning for me to follow. "We're done here."

For whatever reason, I smiled at Cynda as I passed, not wanting to upset the apex predator in the small room on a ghost ship in the middle of the ocean. I'd seen what she could do, jumping from great heights and ripping people to shreds with her hands. I didn't want to piss her off.

She gave Ben a little hiss as he put a hand on my back

and led me away. It wasn't until we reached the upper deck that I took a full breath and mouthed the word *thank you.* He just nodded. We exchanged no words as we rowed back to The Queen, but Ben sat close and then made sure I got to my room after we returned.

We stood outside my door, and he glanced around. "Are you alright?"

I nodded. "How much of our conversation did you hear?"

"Just the end of it as I crept down the hall," he replied honestly. "And when I saw the look in Cynda's eyes, like a wolf narrowing in on its prey…." He shook his head and loosed an angry sigh.

A shiver rocked me, and Ben's hands were on my arms, rubbing warmth into me.

"Would you…stay with me?" I dared ask. "In case she…."

He paused for a moment. "Of course."

I opened the door and let him inside the little eighty-square-foot space. "Don't worry, I won't throw myself at you again."

We laughed as he shut the door, and I removed my jacket. I'd kill for a warm bath. The pirate life was the grimy life, and I wondered how my mother coped with it. She was a renowned chef and a skilled baker; cleanliness just came with the territory with her. Our house was always spotless.

"What are you doing?" I asked Ben as he eased into the little chair across from the bed. He just looked at me, aghast. "Aren't you going to sleep?"

He had to have been as exhausted as me. My bones hurt.

"I can sleep here," he said, noticing how uncomfortable the wooden chair was.

I rolled my eyes. "So, you're just going to sit and stare at me like a weirdo?"

His brows pinched together. "Weirdo?"

My heart skipped a beat. That wasn't a common saying here. "Uh, someone insane?"

Ben just stared at me for a moment, something like a memory in his eye. He shook it away and glanced at the chair beneath him. "Very well."

I slid under the handmade quilt, holding it open for him as he kicked off his boots and climbed in with me. I wanted to melt into him, not just because of the damp chill that always soaked our clothes at sea, but because… it was *Ben*. But I couldn't, because this wasn't my Ben, he didn't know me.

Ben from the future knew my favorite ice cream flavor, that I dipped French fries in chocolate shakes, and that I hated pickles on anything. He knew I'd spent my childhood avoiding the sea and filled my time with karate, rock climbing, gymnastics, and dance.

I couldn't seek solace in this man. He was practically a stranger to me.

So, instead, I lay on my side and stared at him, my hands and arms clenched to my chest. We lay silently for a while, listening to the ship breathing and the ocean crashing against her sides. He stared at the ceiling in my tiny room, those warm brown eyes lost in thought. I couldn't possibly sleep. I felt electric just lying next to him. Even through centuries of time, something in me reached for him.

Finally, he loosed a sigh but held his stare above. "I have a confession to make."

My pulse quickened. "What's that?"

"I heard your conversation with Cynda."

"All of it?" My mouth ran dry.

Ben craned his neck and looked at me, examining my face as if looking for something specific. "Yes, all of it."

"Then why did you help me?" I asked. "I thought you hated sirens."

"First of all, I do hate those beasts." He shook his head at some memory. "But you're not a siren. You're just cursed by them, and I know better than anyone that it's not your fault."

But it kind of was. I had been a naïve, foolish child and made a stupid wish. Would the siren have found a way to curse me if I hadn't done that? Was it her plan all along?

"I'm still…figuring it all out," I replied quietly. "I don't know what it means, for me, my life. I wish there was—"

Ben cupped a hand over my mouth, eyes wide, and for a second, panic filled me. But he smiled and gently removed his hand.

"Don't ever use that word," he warned jokingly.

We chuckled together, and I pulled the blanket up around my neck as I tried not to let the chill sink deeper. The warmth of his body was like a heating pad, and I just wanted to burrow in his arms. But I had to stop. I had to watch my actions around him. I couldn't imagine how confusing it must be for him to have this strange woman suddenly appear and look at him the way I did.

"I'm sorry about my behavior earlier," I told him. "I was delirious."

Ben chuckled softly. "You're forgiven." His eyes fell to my lips. "It wasn't exactly unpleasant."

"Why'd you push me away then?" I teased, unable to help myself.

"Aside from the dead body?" He grinned at my eye roll but then drifted in thought. "I'm trying to break old habits. I have a horrible history of…jumping in head-first when women show me any bit of kindness. And it's gotten me nowhere. I'm still alone. I need to find my place in this world before sharing it with someone."

Fuck it. I reached across the few inches between us,

cupped his cheek in my hand, caressing my thumb over his beard, and smiled as our eyes met.

"You will…" I swallowed dryly and blinked away the wetness that formed around my eyes. "I promise you will." He covered my hand with his and seemed to relish in the touch as those eyes never blinked, never strayed from mine.

It just takes three hundred years.

CHAPTER SIXTEEN

I slammed to the floor and jolted awake, unable to find my footing. The ship felt like it was going to tip over! I grabbed hold of the bedframe and steadied myself. Ben was gone. The door hung open, flapping about as the ship rocked back and forth.

We must be in a storm.

I managed to stumble into the narrow hallway and made my way through the swaying beast, knocking into crates and fumbling over fallen debris. Where the hell was everybody?

"Ace?"

I spun around. "Kiri!"

She hugged the walls and fought against the gravity that threw us both around. "What's going on?"

"I think it's a storm," I said as she slammed into me.

Something groaned beyond the thin walls of the ship's belly, and all the hairs on my arms became electrified. Kiri looked up at me, eyes wide with fear, and slowly shook her head.

"I spent months on a ship before–" Something groaned again, deeper, louder, and more aggressive. "That's not a storm."

A loud crash followed by a man's howl sent my heart racing. I gripped the dagger still strapped to my thigh. "We have to go up there!"

"Are you mad?"

"You should return to your room and lock the door," I said sincerely. "Don't come out until the rocking stops."

Kiri hesitated. How could I fault her if she wanted to go back? Christ, she was a kid. To me, anyway. Here, in the past, she was practically a woman at sixteen. I needed her to go to her room and wanted nothing more than for her to be safe. But I also wouldn't dare tell her what to do.

She finally sighed, frustrated, and pried open a crate from the stack we leaned against in a corner. Rum. She opened another box. Pistols, accompanied by three smaller boxes. Lead ammo and gunpowder.

We gave each other a curt nod and loaded three guns.

One for me and two for Kiri.

"Are you sure you want to do this?" I asked her once more. "Staying safe is also being brave, you know."

"I may very well become someone's wife, someone's mother," she replied. "And I welcome it. But for now...." She cocked a pistol in each hand. "My father taught me to shoot for a reason. Let's see what the hell's going on up there."

Another cry from someone had us running through the ship and up ladders to the upper deck. Blood slickened the wood, threatening to take my feet out from beneath me, but utter disbelief held me in place as I stared up at a massive, thick black tentacle falling through the air.

I grabbed Kiri and dove out of the way just as it hit the deck and swiped across it. Something eclipsed the moon above, casting a shadow over us, and I peered up in horror as one long, obsidian appendage gripped Eric around his torso, and he screamed in pain as the kraken squeezed him fifty feet in the air.

Without a second thought, Kiri began firing her pistols at the thicker base of the arm, and I took a deep breath before joining her. I got closer, so my dagger could hack at the beast, but Eric let out a gurgled cry of pain as the kraken tightened its grip.

"We're just making it angrier!" I shouted. "It's going to kill him! Where the hell is everyone?"

Through the chaos, I spotted Lottie lying unconscious in a corner, her body covered in blood I prayed wasn't hers. Finn let out fierce battle cries as he swung his mighty broadsword, kraken meat flying all around him.

"Cynda's in the water!" Finn yelled.

The ship tipped again, groaning under pressure, and one of the wooden planks snapped, followed immediately by another. Two more tentacles emerged from the water and crashed onto the deck, smashing the railing and swiping back and forth as the beast attempted to wipe us from the ship.

"Where's Ben?" I called out to Finn, and he looked back at me with crazed eyes and a blood-slicked face.

"Cannons!" he shouted back and dove out of the way of a curled tentacle.

I sliced the tip off with my dagger, hitting the deck with a heavy, moist sound. "Why is the kraken attacking us? I thought it was guarding Solomon's grave?!"

Finn stumbled toward Kiri and me, and the three of us stood between the chaos and Lottie, protecting our captain.

"I dinnae know," Finn said with a huff, his shoulders tense and his chest heaving with wet breaths. "We're close, but nae that close. It's almost as if it knew we were comin'."

Just then, Cynda shot out of the water like a rocket

and landed on the deck with a graceful stomp, her black curls hanging loose and wet around her. Blood and yellow goo dripped down her arms as she turned to us with crazed eyes.

"I've blinded it," she informed. "But the fucking beast won't let Eric go!"

Right on cue, Eric let out another gurgled scream, matched with the shriek that came from beneath the ship. The kraken was pissed off now that Cynda tore out its eye, but the creature had eight arms, and there was only a handful of us.

"We need to get to the arm that's holding him," I said.

"Aye," Finn added. "We're tryin', lass. But the beasty won't let us near."

A loud boom rocked the ship, and the wood vibrated beneath my feet. The cannons. Ben must have gotten them armed. The sea creature's grip on our ship loosened, and Eric's body fell to the deck as tentacles slithered away and the beast writhed next to us, splashing in the water, pushing massive waves onto the deck that threatened to wash us all away.

We all held on to something and each other and stood over Lottie's body as the sound of wood smashing sent my heart racing even faster.

Iron groaned in the air, and another tentacle swung toward us, gripping one of the giant cannons in its coil.

"Hit the deck!" Cynda shouted, her arms extended around us.

We fell to the ground, the heavy iron cannon narrowly missing us as it crashed into the wall of the captain's quarters. Wood splintered around us, deafening my ears, and the tentacle slowly retreated to the water.

My head snapped to Finn; his eyes were already wide with alarm.

"Ben!" we both said in unison.

I took off running for the decks below, unsure where the cannons were exactly, slamming into walls as I took sharp corners in panic.

"Ben!" I called frantically. "Ben!"

"Ace!" I heard him reply and quickened my feet as I ran toward the sound.

I threw myself into a swinging door and landed in an open space with cannons on either side. Giant iron balls rolled across the floor, where Ben shoved to his feet in front of a giant hole in the ship's side.

I nearly cried at the sight of him, safe and sound, and he smiled as I ran to him. But the kraken was faster. I choked on my heart as Ben jolted backward, the tip of a black tentacle yanking at his waist, ripping him through the hole in the ship.

I leaped forward, arm outstretched toward nothing. He was gone in an instant.

There was no time to stand around and think, let alone run up above for help. I darted for the hole, lungs burning, and paused for half a second, long enough to take a deep breath.

And then I jumped into the sea.

My body sank through the dark, jade depths, propelling down, down, down as flurries of bubbles passed me. A trail leading me right to Ben. I couldn't think about the fact that I didn't know how to swim back to the surface or think of the crippling fear of the sea that had gripped me my entire life.

The water turned frigid, and the bubbles disappeared. My body began to drift back toward the surface, and my lungs begged for air. *No, please*, I thought. *I have to find him.*

I cursed my inability to swim and the useless body that could do everything else yet couldn't fucking *swim*.

But maybe I could.

Siren blood ran in my veins. I'd wished for it to be like them, beautiful, terrifying, agile, and powerful. Where was all that now? Where did it all hide within me?

As the last of the oxygen died in my lungs, my body clenched, threatening to convulse, but then melted and softened inside as some foreign sensation filled me. Suddenly, I didn't need to breathe, and my skin felt warm as it hummed with new life.

Okay, I thought. *Now to swim.*

But not like a human. No, I had to cross the sea like a siren and find my way to Ben. I remembered, vaguely, but it was there, the memory of Seneca taking me and my brother Arthur when we were four. She moved through the oceans of time at hyper speed.

A shadow moved through the water, circling in the distance. I knew it wasn't the kraken, it was far too small. Another shadow moved to my right.

Show yourselves, cowards.

Two forms approached, and something inside me recognized them. *Felt* them. Like I was part of the sea now, too. Even my eyes were slowly changing, adjusting like a camera coming into focus, and suddenly the ocean was a sprawling landscape before me.

You've broken the rules, Audrey Cobham.

No, I haven't.

Strange, echoed shrieks filled my ears. *You've revealed who you are to someone.*

Finn? I replied through my mind. *No, he guessed my identity. I had no part in that.*

There are no loopholes in the game, Audrey Cobham. We'll give you a second chance, but not without a cost.

Impatience hummed through my limbs. I didn't have time to float here and argue with sirens. I had to find Ben before the kraken—*You!* I exclaimed. *The kraken attack, Ben, this was all your doing?!*

The devilish creatures circled me tauntingly. *The price has been paid*, they said together, and I swear I heard them snicker evilly. *Poor, soft human lungs. A shame they cannot breathe underwater.*

What?!

Rage erupted within me, and I moved without thought, reaching for the dagger strapped to my thigh. I swung toward one of them, slicing right through the otherworldly flesh of her stomach, and she let out an ear-piercing scream as her sister charged at me. I kicked her away, surprised by the brute strength that suddenly moved my muscles.

In one swift movement, I stuck my blade into the other siren's torso and heaved upward, gutting her in the water. Her giant black eyes widened in disbelief as I stared into them, her innards floating in the water around us.

The other siren came bolting back, and I spun around, slicing my blade through the sea and narrowly missing her throat as she halted and pushed away, undiluted anger in her evil eyes.

You'll pay for this crime, Audrey Cobham!

I gripped the handle of the dagger tightly and gritted my teeth. *I've already paid greatly! My family has been paying your price for years! And you won't even tell us why! You stole my childhood! You ruined my grandmother's life and nearly killed my mother! Is that not enough?* I charged at her. *Isn't it?!*

She swiftly grabbed my wrist and yanked me toward

her, our faces touching. *The price is the curse, and it shall never end.*

I would not show fear. I let go of my dagger, grabbed it with my other hand, and shoved it through her chest. *Then I'll break the curse if I have to gut every siren in the sea.*

As I did to her sister, I dragged my blade through her abdomen and shoved her body away with one hefty kick. I floated there, watching her fade away into the dark depths of the sea as her blood saturated the water.

Something unnatural took hold of me, spilling into my mind. A need. I wanted to kill them all. If no sirens were left in the sea, then there could be no Cobham curse, and my family would finally be free of their devilish meddling.

What about Ben?

It was a distant whisper of my own voice, luring me from the catatonic rage I was sinking into. My heart sprang inside my chest, and I spun around, searching for the right direction. It might be too late; the siren had said the price was paid. But I had to try. I had to find him.

I closed my eyes and searched with my heart, feeling for him in the stark cold surrounding me until I sensed it. A spark of warmth. My new eyes flew open with determination.

Go.

My body bolted through the sea like lightning, knowing exactly where to go. It only took seconds, but I must have traveled a mile before I saw the gargantuan silhouette of the blinded kraken. It couldn't see me coming, but I bet it could feel me in the water.

I darted around it, dodging the seven injured tentacles that already seemed to be healing, and frantically searched for the arm holding the man I loved. The fear that I might have been too late possessed me, but I gasped inwardly as I spotted his limp body dangling in the kraken's grip.

Release him!

The beast roared, shaking the sea, and swung at me. I dodged it and thrust my body closer to where it cradled Ben to its body. Sliding my arms beneath his, I tried to pull him free, but the beast's hold was too strong, so, in desperation, I stuck the tip of my blade into the blubbery flesh and tore a deep gash down the length of it, forcing the creature to loosen its grip.

Another deep caw erupted from the giant, but Ben's lifeless body floated toward me, and I wasted no time. With one arm wrapped around him, I stuck the other out in front of me and willed myself to bolt through the sea once more, sensing where The Queen bobbed on the water. It only took a few moments to reach it, but I knew… he'd been underwater too long.

I broke the surface and clung to the rope ladder that dangled over the side. "*Help!*" I screamed as loud as I could. "Help us!"

"Lass!" Finn said with a frantic mix of surprise and relief as he peered over the edge. He let out a delirious laugh and scrambled over the railing, a rope in his hands, and climbed the ladder. "We thought we'd lost ye–" He stared wide-eyed; the color drained from his face. "Yer eyes…"

I struggled to hold Ben as the magic in my blood faded, and my eyes adjusted to normal. "Help me get him on the ship," I huffed, and Finn quickly tied the rope around Ben's torso, tucking it under his armpits.

Finn whistled up at someone above, and Ben's body began hoisting up the ship's side. We climbed up the ladder next to him, and my muscles screamed. The rapid descent back to mortality was a total punch in the gut.

After gently maneuvering Ben's body over the edge, I collapsed on the deck next to him as Finn and Eric untied the rope. Kraken blood and bits of flesh still covered everything, and the air soured with a fishy reek. But none of that mattered.

I scrambled over Ben's chest and felt for a pulse. Nothing thrummed against my trembling fingertips. I tipped his chin up, cleared his airways, and flew into CPR, not caring that the concept didn't exist in this time. I had to save him.

I opened his mouth and blew air into his lungs, pumping his chest again and again and again.

"What is she doing?" Eric muttered.

"Resuscitation," Finn replied. "I've seen it before."

I flicked a quick look up at him, and he threw me a wink. My mother must have shown him at some point.

Eric looked down at me with disdain, then lazily glanced at Finn. "Lottie's still unconscious," he said curtly and headed to her quarters as if someone wasn't lying dead on the floor at his feet.

Cold-hearted bastard.

I ignored the world around me as I slipped into a robotic state of chest compressions and inflated Ben's lungs with air from my own. Over and over. I had no idea how much time had passed, but Finn never said a word; he just stood by my side as desperation began to set in. There was no response. He was a corpse.

"No!" I balled his shirt in my fists. "No, you can't leave me!" I screamed in his face as tears streamed down my cheeks, mixing with the salt water that soaked every inch of me.

A hand slid over my shoulder and squeezed gently. "Lass, he's gone."

"No, he can't be," I said and shot a look up at him. I wondered what I looked like if any of the siren form still remained in my eyes as they burned with hot tears. "You don't understand, Finn. If he…" I swallowed the lump in my throat and lowered my voice. "If he dies here, what does that mean for the future Ben? For *my* Ben?"

He crouched beside me. "I dinnae ken, lass. But ye

cannae blame yerself."

I gritted my teeth and cut a seething look out toward the sea. "I don't. I blame the monsters that did this."

I pushed to my feet, secured my dagger in its sheath, and took a deep breath.

"Audrey, what are ye doin'?" he said, realization seeping into his voice. He shot to his feet and grabbed my arm. "Don't."

"I have to," I replied. "What other choice do I have? I can't let him die here."

"Ye cannae let yerself get further mixed up with those wretched things. They'll ruin yer life."

I sighed. "They already have." I tipped my chin toward Ben's body. "Watch him for me. I'll be back soon."

Filling my lungs, I sprinted toward the edge, jumped over the railing, and dove into the frigid sea. I searched within me for that strange, otherworldly spark and dug it up from the burrows of my gut, willing it to cooperate. Within moments, my skin changed, my lungs transformed, and my eyes adjusted. The great expanse of the underwater world came into focus, and I called out with my mind.

I demand to speak with you!

Nothing happened.

Bring me to your mother!

A shadow approached, and I realized then that it wasn't

really a shadow but a formless entity moving through the water as if part of it. The siren stopped a few feet away, leery as it solidified before me.

Don't you mean our *mother?* it said in an eerie musical tone, baring its pointed teeth.

I'm nothing like you, I didn't ask for any of this.

Oh, but you did, the creature replied. *And look how well it suits you, Audrey Cobham.*

I gripped the handle of my knife, and she took note, a low hiss coming from some part of her. *Bring. Me. To. Your. Mother. Now.*

As you wish, she replied darkly and wrapped her clawed, webbed hand around my arm.

Instantly, we melted away, becoming one with the sea, and we traveled so fast my eyes couldn't relay the images to mind quick enough. I felt sick and nearly hurled as she came to a screeching halt by an underwater waterfall that seemed to defy the laws of science as I knew it.

What is—she thrust me forward, and I fell through the waterfall, landing on a slick rock surface in a hollow cavern filled with air that stretched on for at least a hundred feet.

I took a moment to collect myself, to let my spinning brain stop and my stomach settle. Glowing pools of silver light lined a stone path toward the cavern's end, where it seemed to veer to the right. Slowly, I pushed to my feet, my knees weak, and carefully strolled along.

Strange melodies echoed off the walls hewn of dark reddish rock, almost lulling me toward sleep. I shook my head, scattering the sleepy thoughts. Before I reached the end, where it began to curve, I stopped and peered into one of the glowing pools.

The silvern light cooled my face, and I stared in awe at my reflection. Eyes of pure sterling, skin that glowed with an iridescent sheen. I looked both stunning and terrifying at the same time.

My reflection faded away, and I noticed tiny serpent-like fish dancing in elegant circles. No…not fish.

Baby sirens.

There were dozens of tiny pools filled with the young of the monsters that plagued my family, and I realized… this was the siren's den. My first thought was revenge. I could kill every last one of these wretched creatures before they could become the beasts I knew all too well. But, as I reached a hand inside the silver water, they swam in and out of my fingers, brushing their silky scales against my strange siren skin; I knew I couldn't.

"Please don't grow up to be monsters like your mother and sisters," I whispered to them. "You have an eternity to do good for the world."

The eerie melody dancing in the air changed from a lulling sound to more of a beckoning, and I headed for the bend in the cavern. The space narrowed in shadow and opened to a massive room with gentle waterfalls and steaming pools where sirens lounged. Curtains of seaweed covered entrances to other tunnels, and another siren sat atop a throne made of rock, her lovely tail pooling to the side like a gown. She was different than all the rest with her thick, kelp hair and those eyes—still large and purely black but anchored with something more human, as if she possessed the conscience and wisdom of the world, unlike her sisters and offspring.

"Audrey Cobham," she spoke my name with a reverent tone. "To what do I owe the pleasure of this visit?"

"I come to ask for a wish pearl," I replied, cutting right to the chase. I had no time to waste.

Her dark brows rose as she clutched her neck and feigned surprise. "You dare come here, to *my* home, and ask a grand favor after what you've done?"

Anger rose within me, but I couldn't fight with her now, not when so much hung on the line. "Please." It killed me to beg her. "The man I love is dead."

She began playing with her hair aloofly. "I care not for the pitiful mortal lives of men."

"He's not mortal, though," I told her. "Benjamin once traded his soul to your kind to help save another. He's a good man. He doesn't deserve to die."

Those lethally dark eyes studied me, and I swore she could hear my heart thrumming wildly in my chest. I hated that I needed her. The mother slowly leaned to the side, dipped her long arm through a glowing pool, and scooped out a handful of pearls. She looked at me with a coy grin, revealing sharp, jagged teeth.

"And what do you have to trade for this precious gift?" she asked. "You've already given your soul for the gift you possess in your blood. What more could you possibly have to offer me?"

My heart stilled. "Wait…is *that* what you took?" I couldn't bottle up the rage any longer. "You took my fucking soul? I was a *child*!"

Her ethereal face morphed with spite and a warning, and she let the pearls fall back into the water. "Watch your tone, Audrey Cobham. You may be immortal, but you are not invincible."

I sucked in a shuddering breath and willed my nerves to calm as tears strained to be set free. *Everything*, they'd ruined *everything*, *taken* everything from me. But I still needed her.

"Please," I said again with a tremble in my voice. "I'll do anything. I'll play whatever games you want me to. Just help me save him."

"You're already playing a game and failing horribly," she reminded.

"How—"

"Need I remind you of the rules?"

"I swear, I've told no one who I really am," I explained. "Finn just knew. I never could have hidden my identity from him. I already told your sisters that."

"The sisters you murdered?"

"They were going to kill me and stop me from saving the man I loved! What would you have done in my place?"

She arched a single brow and pursed her wide mouth. "The same man who knows of your blood?"

"That's not *who* I am," I defended. "There's no rule against telling people *what* I am, only *who* I am." I reeled back, taking a deep breath to calm myself. I clenched my fists. "Look. I'm doing everything I can to play your stupid game and get home. I swear. I'm doing what you've asked of me, I found my parent's old friends, and they'll help me get home, but I have to help them get to Solomon's grave and get Endor Stone first. But I can't do anything if Ben dies. I…can't go back to a future without him."

"Forget about the relic," she spat, leaning over her throne towards me. "Just finish the game and go home, child. The quest these people have you on will not lead to good things."

"Like you know what good is," I chortled.

She gave me a challenging stare. "I know what evil looks like, and that's all that matters."

"Evil is bidding a naïve child's wish and stealing her mortality–"

"Stealing!" she balked and straightened her back as gills flexed along her neck. "You begged us for that wish. You came to the sea every night, taunting, demanding the sirens for immortality. Your time with Seneca enamored you. You wanted it so badly that you dreamed of it every night. Immortality, the magic, the power. So, we finally granted it, not to be cruel but to be rid of you!" She pretended to examine her nails. "But a gift such as that comes with a price, a curse if you will." She curled a finger at me, and her gaze darkened. "You live forever, but those you love do not."

"I was a child!" Tears stung the rims of my eyes. "Why do you hate us so much? Why haunt the Cobhams like you do? What have we ever done to you that's so horrible? My mother risked her life to return your heart. Wasn't that enough?"

I watched breathlessly as she scooped her hand through the water again. This time…I noted *how* she did it. The energy, the movements, the way she took a breath and held it for a second too long.

She dropped the pearls back into the water.

"I gifted your mother kindly." She stared at me coldly. "She wasn't like the Cobham women I once knew. She's good, down to her core, and she loves deeply. She did what her mother before her could not, and her selfless act returned my heart and restored my people. But it doesn't erase what was done so many years ago."

I shrugged tightly. "What was done?"

She was silent. Unblinking.

I craned my neck forward, holding her stare. "*What was done?*"

She tilted her head. "Centuries ago, a siren was in love with a man, a Cook man. Your Benjamin's ancestor. He pretended to love her, and she gave him treasures, making him wealthy beyond anyone's dreams."

My pulse thrummed in my ears.

"But he fell in love with a human woman, one of three Cobham sisters, and broke the siren's heart. Then, fearing what she might do, he killed her in cold blood on the beach one fateful night after luring her onto land with the sweet promise of a kiss."

My eyes watered over as I skipped ahead and realized how this story had ended.

"He then fed her flesh to his aristocratic acquaintances." The mother siren gritted her teeth. "You call us beasts, yet humans are capable of such insidious things."

"Ben's ancestor…and…mine?" *Were we related?* My stomach churned.

She waved boredly. "Do not fret, Audrey Cobham. Benjamin Cook's bloodline never had the chance to cross with yours. I cursed your ancestors myself for what was done to my sister and drove yours into the sea." She lifted her pointed chin smugly. "The Cook bloodline shall never feel the love of a human woman, and the Cobham line is cursed to eternal heartbreak."

And there it was. The answer my mother and grandmother had been asking for decades. *Why?* Why torture the Cobham women so much?

"I…I shouldn't have to pay for the mistakes of my ancestors. So, what? This *never* ends? We just fight, my people and yours, for the rest of eternity?" She was blank and unmoving, but something flickered in those black, alien eyes. A glimmer of hope, perhaps? "I'm sorry for what was done, then and now. And all I can do is offer a truce, to swear to never harm your kind again. But you have to meet me halfway." When she still didn't reply, I pressed on. "I didn't wish to be like you. I only wished for immortality. Your lot chose to make me like you for a reason. You can't deny that much. And I believe it was a step forward, a way to bridge the gap."

The slight change in her expression and the twitch of malice gave me all the necessary answers. Some of her kin wanted to end this centuries-old curse.

I smiled as I filled with contentment and reached into my pocket, plucking my blood pearl. "I'm done playing the game. I don't need you to revoke my wish anyway. I think I'll keep it." I dropped the pearl back into my jacket pocket, and her mouth gaped wordlessly. I just gave her a shit-ass grin and a brazen salute. "And I'll spend eternity fighting to free my family from your stupid curse."

Her look of shock only lasted a moment before her expression filled with something devious. "So, you forfeit the game?"

"I never wanted to play in the first place."

"What of another game, then?"

My brows pinched together. "Are you serious? Nothing would ever make me play another of your twisted plots again."

She made a show of bending to the side, leaning over her throne to another glowing pool, dipping her hand inside the sparkling waters, and pulling out a palm-sized stone. No, not a stone. Some sort of amulet, a rough-cut emerald cast in a border of patinaed gold.

She pinched it between her fingers, taunting me with it. "Not even to save the man you love?"

"Is that…" My mouth ran dry.

"The Endor Stone?" She glanced at it with a coy sneer. "The ancient relic your friend seeks to bring back the man *she* loves. But you could use it for your Benjamin."

"That's not fair!"

"Life's not fair," she replied dryly and flung the stone at me. I floundered and caught it. "And neither is eternity."

A deep rumble built beneath my feet, and I searched for the source. The mother siren just sneered with a grin, a frightening beauty lounging on her throne of stone, deviously waiting for…something.

Suddenly, water came from all around, pouring and blasting through cracks and holes, shooting right for me. A gasp froze in my chest, and I widened my legs, bracing for impact. The last thing I did as the water crushed me from every direction was cut a death stare toward the mother siren before I washed away.

The ravaging sea ripped me from where I stood and carried me from the siren's den, spitting me back into the vast, frigid ocean. I fought against the tide that spun me in circles and grasped the Endor Stone firmly in my hand. Finally, everything slowed to a manageable current, and I gained my bearings. Like a fuzzy star, the faintest yellow light glowed on the surface, and I shot toward it.

I grabbed the rope ladder and stuffed Solomon's relic in my jacket pocket. How the hell was I going to resurrect Ben without Lottie noticing I was using the very thing she wanted? I'd have to make a show of diving for the grave and pretend it was empty. Then there was the fact that I had zero ideas how to even use the thing, which meant breaking into Lottie's quarters and stealing from her.

She was going to kill me.

The lower half of my body was still in the water. I gripped the rope and pressed my forehead against it as tears spilled over. *Life's not fair, and neither is eternity.* What a fucking bitch. Everything seemed so impossible, so much bigger than me, resurrecting the dead, trying to find a way to travel home to the future.

"I just want to go home," I sobbed to myself.

But I refused to leave without Ben. I *had* to do everything I could. I climbed the rope once again as the magic dissipated or retreated to some dark place inside me…I wasn't sure. I struggled over the edge and rolled onto the deck, breathless.

"Lass?" Finn said curiously. I sat up, and he gave me a look that was a question in itself. I shook my head, and he slumped where he sat on a crate, Kiri at his side with her knees to her chest. Ben's body was right where I had left it. I couldn't bring myself to look directly at him.

Solomon's rock burned in my pocket, begging to be used. If only I knew how.

I lay down next to Ben, my face to the stars above, my hands at my sides. The sky swayed like a navy blanket, and as I stared at it, I'd never felt so lost.

Lottie was still unconscious, and I didn't want to imagine how she would react to the news about Cynda. And Eric didn't seem to give a shit about anything at all.

Something cold trickled by my fingertips, and I sat up. Water flowed across the deck in a moving puddle toward Ben. My breath held still in my throat as I watched it rise and morph into a mermaid. *The* mermaid, the one that had helped me before. Free from the sea, she looked more…

real. Tangible.

Finn leaned forward, tense, his hand on his sword. She turned and looked at me from over her shoulder, large dark eyes blinking at me. Not as large as a siren's, and different, not void of humanity. Her thick tail faded away into the water, trailing to the edge from where she crawled.

"What are you doing?" I asked her.

"Helping," she replied before moving over Ben's body.

Her strangely long fingers pried open his mouth, covering it with hers. I couldn't look away, couldn't even blink. His chest rose and fell with three slow breaths from her, and she gently pulled away as she sat up and looked down at him with kindness.

The air was still and silent as we waited for a beat. Ben suddenly coughed, arching his back from the floor, and only then did I take a breath of my own. My eyes stung as I finally blinked.

"Bloody Christ," Finn whispered. "Now I've seen it all."

I wrapped my hands around the back of his head, cradling it as he coughed up water. I turned him to the side, and the rest spewed onto the wooden planks. I held him tight from behind and sobbed into his shirt.

I craned my neck to look at the mermaid, my cheek to Ben's back as he continued coughing up the sea. "Thank you," I told her. "Thank you so much."

She leaned in, her face just inches from mine, and rested

her delicate hand on my arm. "Break the curse and set us all free."

"What—"

As I caught my own reflection in her eyes, I saw it. I saw the mirror of my bloodline flashing through her gaze. Could see it in her heart-shaped face and curls of kelp. The way she carried her shoulders, even in this form.

"You," I said in a cold whisper. "You're the one they drove into the sea."

She smiled kindly and tilted her head, taking me in one last time as she sunk into a puddle and poured off the ship back into the sea.

Break the curse and set us all free.

The curse that began with her. The Cook bloodline never feels the love of a human woman, and the Cobham line suffers an eternity of heartbreak.

But I wasn't entirely human, and I loved Ben with everything that made me.

Ben groaned and rolled back toward me, his usually tanned skin now parlor but alive. *Alive.*

"Hey, Ace," he said hoarsely, then his forehead wrinkled as life trickled back into his eyes. "I thought you couldn't swim?"

A maddened laugh erupted from me, and I crushed him in my arms. Anything. I could face *anything* now that he was alive.

Including destroying this generational curse once and for all.

CHAPTER SEVENTEEN

BEN

I pried my eyes open to meet the dimly lit room around me and rubbed a hand over my face and beard, noting the dried sea salt crusted to the hairs. From how the ship swayed in place, I knew the sails were down. Images of everything suddenly came flooding back.

Being thrown from the bed, ripped from Ace's arms. Securing her inside the room while I ran up on deck. The slick, wet sounds of the kraken's tentacles crashing against the ship. From there…things turned muddy. I vaguely remembered bolting down to the cannons to free the ship from the kraken's hold, but…

"Hey, you're awake," Ace spoke from a chair in the

corner of my room. She looked tired—no…she looked like she'd been crying.

"How long was I out?" Everything hurt to move.

"A few hours," she replied, exhaustion soaking her tone. She moved to the edge of the chair, her eyes bright and glossy, watching me wearily.

"Thank you for saving me."

A sad look washed over her. "I didn't save you. The mermaid did."

"No, you saved me," I said. "In the water. I remember."

"What?" Her face paled. "How did—you were unconscious."

"The kraken's hold around my body was tight, and the air had burned up in my lungs. I was ready to give up and let it win when I saw you cutting through the water. Your eyes…they glowed like moonlight."

She cringed. "You saw that?"

"I thought it was a dream," I told her and laughed. The huff of air burned my raw throat, and she scooted onto the bed. "I'm fine," I assured her, and her hands fell to her lap as if she weren't sure what to do with them. I slid my hand across the blanket and braided my fingers with hers. "So, you really are like them."

"A monster?" Ace quipped. "Yes."

Lord, is that how she saw herself? A word I so often used to describe myself. I gently pulled at her hand, coaxing her closer, and cradled her face with my palm. "No, magnificent."

I couldn't ignore the way she melted into my touch, as if she'd been waiting for it. This glorious being, sitting on my bed, who'd risked everything to save me. I'd been so wrapped up in my own mind about not wanting to repeat old mistakes that I didn't see what was right in front of me.

My equal. Another immortal.

"What possessed you to jump in like that when you knew you couldn't swim?"

Her dark eyes filled with tears, and she pressed her mouth into a thin line. "When…when the kraken burst through the side of the ship and took you, I didn't–I couldn't think of anything else. I just jumped."

"Well, I guess we're both lucky your curse happened to come with that ability, then."

She smiled and squeezed our joined hands as she blew out a jittered breath. She was barely holding on, her seams were ripping, and I wanted nothing more than to hold her together. I moved closer to the wall and opened the blanket.

"Get in," I said. When she hesitated, I added, "I'm cold. I could use the body heat."

Ace tossed her coat on the chair and crawled under the blanket without a word. We lay there, facing one another, our warm breaths entwined, our gazes locked just as we did the night before. She was, without a doubt, the most beautiful thing I'd ever seen. But Ace's beauty wasn't what drew me in, or the fact that she endured a siren's curse.

It was her undiluted bravery in this unforgiving world. The way she'd jumped aboard a pirate crew with no experience just to find a way home after escaping her enemies. How she ran tearing through Nassau to save Kiri. And how she'd leaped into the sea to save me, despite being unable to swim.

I'd been searching all these years for my purpose, for what made me happy. And she was lying right in front of me. Because, when I looked in her eyes…I saw it. Everything that I could have; happiness and love and an eternity of it.

Before I could talk myself out of it, I leaned in and kissed her.

She gripped my wrists, pulling my hands from her face. "Ben, what are you–"

I kissed her again.

"Wait," she said as her lips moved against mine. "Are you sure? You're hurt."

I pulled back and put my forehead to hers. "I've never been more sure of anything in my life."

She grinned against my mouth. "Well, then, Benjamin Cook. I'm all yours."

I moaned and tightened my arms around her. "I love

how you say my name."

She chuckled to herself and shook her head before peeling back the blankets and climbing on top of me. "Better let me take it from here," she said, splaying those beautiful hands over my chest. "What, with you recovering from death and all."

I dug my fingers into her thighs, barely able to contain myself, and squared my jaw. "Yes, ma'am."

CHAPTER EIGHTEEN

AUDREY

I had no idea what time it was, but morning must have come. I could hear the sounds of the ship coming alive, sails hoisting, and Finn bellowing from above. Kiri must have already been in the kitchen for a while. The smell of breakfast cooking had lured me awake.

But I didn't want to move. Ben's thick arms banded around me, holding me tight to his warm body as we nestled beneath the blanket. Last night was a turning point in my life. Majorly.

I'd discovered why the sirens hated the Cobham women so much and that Ben's life was inextricably en-twined with mine through our ancestors' actions. And

I alone possessed the ability to break the generational curse that poisoned our bloodlines by merely loving him. I wanted to utter the words so many times last night, but I couldn't. Not here, not for this Ben. I'd love any version of him, but this Ben still needed time to grow, years to figure things out after I left.

Because I was going to leave. I would figure out a way home, and one day I'd be gone from here. I couldn't tell Ben I loved him. I couldn't tell him anything at all for fear of how that knowledge might affect the future. Already, I'd done too much simply by being here, seeing him, and being with him. These memories didn't exist for my Ben until now. What was he doing in the future as these images suddenly poured in?

Was that even how it worked?

Sighing, I quietly slipped from the bed and put on my clothes. But I wasn't quiet enough.

"Hey, Ace," Ben croaked tiredly and rolled over to face me with a smile. The blanket fell to his waist, revealing his toned and muscled body that had ravaged me all night. "Where you off to?"

"I have to talk to Lottie about something," I replied, hovering over him for a kiss. "Plus, with Cynda gone, I'm betting Finn needs help."

He sat upright. "What do you mean Cynda's gone?"

Right. He wasn't there. "When you were down below,

with the cannons, the kraken…tore her in half."

"Cynda's *dead*?"

I nodded, trying not to let the graphic memory shape my mind.

Ben flung the blanket off, and his bare feet hit the floor.

"What are you doing?" I asked.

"Lottie and Finn are going to need all the help they can get," he said, searching for his pants. "Cynda was our muscle. Plus–" He stopped and sighed. "Shit."

"What?"

He stared at me, then look at the door with a distant gaze, as if looking all the way to Lottie's room. "She was supposed to dive for Solomon's grave."

"Don't worry," I told him. "I've got that covered."

He grabbed me by the hips and pulled me toward him, staring up at me with admiration. "Of course you do. Just full of surprises, aren't you, my siren?"

My siren. I would have grimaced at the name before. But coming from his lips, with such love in his voice, it melted me. I *was* his. I held his face in both hands and kissed him. "We'll see."

I went upstairs and nodded at Finn across the deck as he coiled thick rope in a loop around his shoulder and arm. The morning mist had yet to burn up with the rising sun, and I wrapped my arms tightly around my torso as I stopped at Lottie's door. I took a deep breath and knocked.

"Come in," she called from the other side.

I twisted the brass knob and entered the captain's quarters. She stood with her back to me behind her big, cluttered desk. I waited until she half-turned and glanced at me. The gash on her head was nearly healed, probably thanks to Eric's magical abilities. But I noticed how she nursed her side as she took a seat.

"Ace," she said. "What can I do for you?" She pretended to fiddle with some parchments in front of her.

"I need your help to get home," I said.

"Yes, I told you. After I get what I need, I can take you anywhere you want."

I took two long strides to her desk and set The Endor Stone on top of a stack of books. Lottie stared at it, her expression unreadable.

"There," I told her. "You don't need a vampire. Take the stone, resurrect Gus, and take me to see The Keepers."

"Cynda was my friend—" Her face drained of all color, and she dragged her eyes from the stone to meet mine. "The Keepers?" I nodded. "The Keepers of *Time*?"

"Yes, they're the only ones who can help me get home."

Denial was written all over her face. Could she truly not admit it to herself?

"And how are The Keepers going to help you get home? Where exactly are you from?"

I placed both palms on her desk and slowly leaned

forward, easing my face closer to hers. Those saddened blue eyes were rimmed with tears and endless sleepless nights.

"I think you already know, Lottie. You've always known."

A single tear spilled over and trailed down her pale cheek. Her mouth fell open, ready to speak, when someone stomped into the room from behind me, stealing her attention. She stood straight and quickly wiped her face with her hand.

"Eric," she said, steeling herself. She tossed him the stone. "Plans have changed."

He fumbled to catch it and cupped the relic with both hands, staring down at it. It was the first time I'd seen him actually make an expression other than discontent. His mouth quirked at the corner, and a low chuckle hummed in his chest. But as he raised his gaze to our captain, there was malice in his eyes.

He spun around and left.

"Eric?" Lottie called after him, but he kept walking away. She looked at me, confused, and I shrugged. I followed her out onto the deck. "Eric!" she said again, but he was muttering something to himself, words in another language. "We have everything we need now. What are you doing?"

"Almost everything," he replied with annoyance and

continued chanting.

Ben appeared from a ladder hatch, Kiri right behind him. He walked over and stopped at my side.

"What's going on?" he whispered.

I shook my head. "I have no idea."

Eric repeatedly chanted, sounding almost Gaelic, and lifted his palm to face the sea before us. Slowly, he moved it in a circle and switched his chant to another Gaelic phrase as a rip formed in the air just a few yards in front of The Queen.

"Eric!" Lottie spat his name. "What the hell is going on?"

He ignored her as the rip expanded, forming a massive hole in space and time. Beyond it, I could see a landscape taking shape. Lush rolling hills and rocky shores. Our ship sailed right for it. Ben wrapped one arm around Kiri and another around me as he held us close.

"Brace yourselves!" Finn called out as the nose of the ship entered the portal.

Everything shook, rattling us off our feet as our red beast sailed through the hole. The masts groaned above like ancient trees swaying in a storm, boards heaved, and crates and ropes slid across the deck, knocking everyone off their feet. I rolled to the side, my body slamming into the railing. And, as the portal finally swallowed the rest of our crumbling ship, everything went dark.

Aside from the pounding of my heart and my breath

in my ears, there was no sight or sound. Someone's hands were on me, helping me to my feet–Ben–I grasped his arm and put my weight against him, but something felt wrong. *He* felt wrong.

It wasn't Ben.

Two strong arms gripped my body, swinging me around and holding me from behind. Cold, hard steel pressed against my throat as the ship's bow tore through the fabric of space and sunlight spilled over the deck, illuminating everything.

Lottie, Finn, Ben, and Kiri struggled to their feet with wide eyes as they took in our new surroundings, unaware that Eric held me prisoner just a few feet behind them.

Finn gargled off a string of Scottish curse words. "We're in *Scotland?*"

Ben and Lottie spotted me, frozen, a blade pushing against the delicate skin of my neck, preventing me from speaking. A mere swallow would surely draw blood.

Ben tensed, ready to charge, but Eric clucked his tongue. "Now, now. Wouldn't want to mar this pretty little neck, would we?"

Lottie narrowed her eyes, fingers wiggling over her bandolier. "Eric, what the *hell* are you doing?"

"Let the lass go," Finn warned.

"Eric," Kiri said, the twinge of betrayal evident in her tone. She'd trusted him, vouched for him when I'd said he was a snake. There were tears in her sweet, innocent eyes. "Don't do this."

He completely ignored her and cut a seething look at the other three. "You foolish mortals. You'll all pay for what you did to my mother."

Ben's eyes never left mine, rage and fear burning within them. Confusion made its way around the group, but Finn chortled. "Yer ma? We've got nae idea who yer ma is, boy."

"Yes, you do," Eric replied. "And *you* know where she's buried."

Finn gave him a scrutinizing look, then something washed over him, realization, and he reeled back, his face gone ghostly white. "Bloody Christ…yer Eric Cobham Jr."

"Surprise."

Lottie removed two knives from her brown leather bandolier. "You're no sorcerer! You just stole the witch's magic!"

"Like you're any better," he replied, clucking his tongue. "Stealing the scrolls of life and death. Thanks for the idea."

She had no reply.

Oh my God… It all made sense now. With his pure disdain for me right off the bat, he must have realized who I was. I rifled through my memories of the facts and stories my parents told me and the things I'd read in the journals. Eric Cobham Jr. was Maria Cobham's son, a boy my dad had saved from her ship when he'd escaped when he was barely a man himself. A boy he'd left with the Keepers to raise.

Kiri looked scared and confused and turned to the others for answers. Lottie never blinked, just fixed her stare on Eric like he was about to drop a precious artifact off the side of a cliff.

"Eric, please," she reasoned. "We can talk about this. We can figure this out. You don't have to hurt her."

His chest vibrated at my back with a sinister laugh. "Oh, I don't plan on hurting her. I never forgot what Captain Barrett did, how he ripped me from my mother and left me with those witches. He thought he was saving me, but he only created a monster. And when I learned that he killed my mother," he stopped to laugh again, a maddening sound, and tightened his grip on me. Ben's fists clenched as desperation held him in place. "I vowed to find a way to kill him." He gently turned the dagger, forcing my chin upward so he could look into my eyes. "But resurrecting my mother and handing her Barrett's daughter to butcher will do just fine."

I couldn't move my head but strained my eyes to look at Ben. He'd gone even whiter, his eyes wide with disbelief. Finn groaned, and Lottie was pure stone as Kiri still stood in a cloud of confusion. The poor thing, I shouldn't have gotten her wrapped up in this mess. I was just trying to save her, but all I did was damn her.

Ben glowered at him, ready to pounce. "Let her go."

Silence hung everywhere.

Eric finally took a deep breath and a step back toward the railing where the ladder hung below. "No."

He tossed me over the edge, and I caught Ben's look of horror as I fell to the rowboat below. I acted instinctually, tucking in my head and limbs just in time as I smacked the wooden seat. The wind knocked from my lungs, and I grasped for a breath. My spine screamed, and I cried out in pain.

"Ace!" everyone called from above.

I could move, despite the searing pain across my lower back. I regained my breath. "I'm…okay!"

Eric appeared on the seat across from me in a poof and rocked the boat. Before I could move, he wrangled me into another chokehold with the dagger.

"Finnigan!" Eric bellowed up to the deck. "Your turn! The rest of you, stay back, or I'll fill this boat with her blood."

A whimper squeezed in my throat as Finn peered over and sighed, then slowly climbed down the rope.

"How did you know?" I dared ask, my skin rubbing across the blade.

"I'm a smart man, observant," Eric said quietly in my ear. "I'm also nosey and have been spying on everyone. I overheard you and Finn talking one day." The boat rocked as Finn took a seat near the back. "Now, let's go raise the dead, *cousin*."

CHAPTER NINETEEN

BEN

My feet nearly slipped out from beneath me as I frantically paced the deck of The Queen. It took every ounce of my resolve not to jump overboard after her, and it killed me, second after second, to watch her drift to shore with that bastard.

"Just wait," Lottie said steadily. "He can't see us follow, or he might kill her."

So many emotions toiled in my chest and burned in my gut.

Kiri cleared her throat. "Can someone please explain to me what's happening?"

Lottie sighed. "Aud—Ace is the daughter of an old

friend of ours…." She paused to exchange a flitting glance with me. "From the future." She swallowed dryly and took a quick breath. "And Eric appears to be the son of our friend's insane sister whom we killed years ago and secretly buried in a jar somewhere in the woods."

Kiri's face was blank as she held herself and backed away. She found a crate to sit on.

My legs were starting to cramp from pacing, and those emotions had bubbled to the surface. I stalked toward Lottie and poked a finger at her chest. "Did you know? Did you *know* when you came crawling to my goddamn door that you had Henry and Dianna's fucking *daughter* with you?"

She just looked guilty as she gnawed at her bottom lip.

I spun away from her, raking my hands through my hair. "Jesus Christ," I whispered. "Why didn't you tell me?"

"I could hardly admit it to myself, Ben. But…how could you *not* see it? I knew immediately. Just *look* at her, for Pete's sake. She's the spitting image of them."

She was right. How did I not see it? Was I blinded by the draw I felt toward her? What was wrong with me? I shot a look toward the rowboat, just a distant speck near the shore now, and blew out a stream of curses.

"She was just a child a few years ago." I felt sick as I spoke the words.

Lottie came to my side and slid a comforting hand over

my shoulders. "Calm down. For her, more than twenty years have passed. She's an adult, Ben, and you had no idea who she was." She bent to catch my distant gaze and gave a reassuring nod. "We'll get her back."

"They're ashore," Kiri noted as she gripped the railing and squinted her eyes.

I wasted no time getting the second rowboat in the water. Lottie emerged from her quarters stacked with weapons and handed me a sword, a dagger, and a pistol. Kiri had two guns and borrowed a warm jacket from Lottie before we scrambled into the boat and rowed ashore. Eric had a decent head start on us, but I wouldn't let that deter me.

We hit the sand, and I leaped from the boat before helping Kiri over the side. When we were on the beach, I scanned the tree line for movement.

"How do we know which direction they went?" Kiri asked. "Do you know where this grave is?"

I shook my head. "No, Finn and Gus were the only ones privy to that information for safety purposes."

"Safety?" she asked, her innocent eyes glistening with worry. "For yourselves?"

"For the world," I told her with finality, and she cowered back. Maria Cobham was the devil incarnate. She could not, under any circumstances, be set free to roam this earth again.

Lottie crouched into a squat and began drawing symbols in the sand.

"What are you doing?" I asked impatiently.

"We don't know where Maria's grave is," she replied and muttered some whisper of a chant. "But I know someone who can tell us." She finished the three symbols, a mix of shapes and lines, and stretched to her feet as she watched the trees.

Within seconds, three shadows emerged, revealing a trio of Keepers, each with varying shades of auburn hair, their bodies draped and wrapped in their usual garb of brown leather and faded green plaid. The one in the middle came forward, her long coat dragging behind her.

"Charlotte Roberts," she said with such authority, her beautiful face taut with a stern look. "You dare summon us after you stole the scrolls of life and death?"

"Apologies," Lottie replied honestly. "But you must understand the desperation that fueled me. I'd do anything to bring back the man I love."

"And what of it?" the Keeper challenged. "How far have you succeeded in your formidable quest to resurrect the dead?"

Lottie squared her jaw, those stormy blues simmering with controlled rage. "I'm closer than you think. I just have to find Eric Cobham jr."

The witch's face hardened. "I thought I sensed him.

We've been tracking Eric for years. He's been using magic to hide his whereabouts, though." She grinned tiredly and lazily dragged her eyes to me. "But we knew he'd be back here at some point."

"Can you help us?" Lottie begged. "Where is Maria Cobham buried? Which direction?"

"I'd bring you there myself," she replied. "But Eric will surely sense me coming. I can portal you to the location." She closed her eyes, and the two women flanking her did the same. She inhaled deeply and slowly looked at us. "He's already there."

I was going to gut the bastard.

The Keeper waved her outstretched palm in the air, much like Eric had on the ship, and a smaller portal opened in the air, revealing a wooded area on the other side.

"There," she said. "Just beyond the trees, you'll find them digging up his mother's ashes. Seize him and call us. We'll come and make sure he's dealt with."

Lottie didn't say a word as she stepped through with determination. I motioned for wide-eyed Kiri to follow and then gave The Keepers a thankful nod as I entered, and the portal closed behind me.

As she'd said, Eric, Finn, and Ace were a few feet beyond the tree line where we stood. Finn was sweating, face red, as he dug into the dirt with his bare hands. Eric watched him like a hawk, Ace in his grasp and held tight from behind, the knife still to her throat. Bits of red clashed with her ivory curls trailing down her neck. Rage seethed in my veins.

He drew her blood.

Lottie placed a gentle but firm hand on my arm. "Don't, not yet. He wants her alive for now. We need to wait until his back is turned."

She let out a quiet whistle of a bird call, and Finn's ears perked. A grin tugged at the corner of his mouth, and he casually glanced around the small clearing they stood in and made a point to land his eyes right in our direction.

Finally, he pulled something from the earth, an old molasses jar, and gave it a sigh before handing it up to Eric. He let his head hang as he shook it sadly. I knew exactly what he was feeling in that moment. Like all of us, we'd made promises to Henry and Dianna, and he'd sworn that Maria would never see the light of day again.

Eric struggled to hold the dagger at Ace's throat and the jar in his other hand, madness in his dark eyes.

"Ye dinnae have to do this, boy," Finn told him. "Ye dinnae ken what type of monster yer ma truly was. I've seen it, with me own eyes, the unspeakable things she's done–"

"You think me a fool?" Eric snapped, his grip on Ace and the jar faltering as he backed away. "I know where we are. I was raised here. I know The Keepers are on their way or perhaps even watching right now." He Set the jar down, forcing Ace to bend with him. She let out a slight whimper, and it took everything in me not to charge at him. He waved his palm in a quick circle, and yet another portal ripped open in the air just inches from him. "But I won't give the satisfaction of catching me."

He snapped his fingers, and Finn's hands became magically bound in front of him, then his ankles behind him. Eric then made the wrong move of trying to force Ace to move with him and grab the jar of his mother's ashes. But she wasn't having it.

"Like Hell, you're taking me through that portal!" Ace grunted as she drove the heel of her boot into his foot.

Eric's grip knocked loose, and she brought her fist upward, colliding with his nose, and he finally released her altogether. Blood gushed down his face as he cupped a hand over his nose and lunged at her with his dagger, forcing her to back up toward the portal.

"We can't let him go through," I whispered frantically to Lottie and Kiri.

Lottie hesitated, but Kiri nodded. "Go, it's now or never."

I rocked forward on the toes of my boots, ready to charge, waiting as Eric bent one more time to retrieve the jar from the ground so his attention wasn't on her and that damned knife. She spun in place, her leg flying outward, and kicked him in the face.

The three of us reeled back in surprise.

"I guess seven years of karate really did come in handy," she said, spitting on him as he cowered on the ground.

But her actions only pissed him off. I caught the slightest movement of his free hand as it searched in the grass for the blade. When his fingers wrapped the worn, leather hilt, I took my chance and ran through the trees.

But I wasn't fast enough. Eric heard me and moved faster than lightning, using magic to grab his mother's ashes and Ace in a split second, and hurdled them through the portal.

"No!" the word tore at my throat.

Lottie and Kiri were there in an instant. The edges of the portal were closing in.

"Help me with Finn!" Lottie yelled.

We each grabbed an arm, and the four of us jumped through the rip in the world, tumbling to the cold, wet sand of a nearby beach. Finn groaned as his bound limbs had him falling on his face, and Lottie barrel rolled to her feet in one swift movement, knives in both hands, ready to fight.

Kiri cocked her pistol and outstretched her arm, aiming right for Eric, but there was no clear shot. Ace squared off with him, blocking every hit and landing her own, unlike anything I'd ever seen. Actually, I had seen it before, the way she moved, the way she used her body weight to both defend and attack. I'd witnessed it in the friends Lottie and I once made in China.

She scuffed the ground as she moved to the side, luring him to mirror and follow, putting his back on me. Lottie expertly flung a knife, landing it in the back of his calf, and he screamed in pain. I wasted no time and wrapped my arms around the man, pinning his arms in place. He wriggled in my grasp, bucking and flailing, and Ace scooped up the jar.

"Stop it!" she cried and held it in the air. Her chest heaved with rapid, exhausted breaths. I'd never been more proud and terrified at the same time. "Stop, or I'll smash your mother's ashes on this beach, and you'll *never* bring her back."

"You, stupid bitch," he spat. "Maybe I *will* gut you myself."

She narrowed her gaze and reeled her arm back in a challenge, ready to spike it on the jagged stones beneath our feet. "I'd like to see you try," she challenged. "You're bound and outnumbered, Eric. Just give up."

His head jolted back, connecting with my face, and I stumbled. Everyone except Finn, who flapped about on the ground like an angry fish, charged at Eric, but he had me in his sights. The sun gleamed off his dagger as he dove at me, driving the blade into my gut.

Air squeezed within my lungs, and my head immediately spun. But I couldn't let him get away. I grabbed his neck and threw him to the ground with every ounce of my weight and strength. The knife twisted in my flesh, but I took his head with both my hands and slammed it into the rocks beneath us repeatedly until his eyes rolled back. Only then did I push to my feet.

I turned and staggered, blood soaking and warming my legs as it gushed around the knife. I plucked it out. The world immediately spun, and I uselessly clapped my palm over the warm hole in my flesh as I searched for one thing, one face among my friends.

CHAPTER TWENTY

AUDREY

Losing the person you love doesn't get any easier the second time around. It felt like Ben hit the ground in slow motion, yet I still couldn't reach him in time. Everything was breaking inside me all at once. My heart, my mind…

"Ben!" I sobbed. Sliding my arm beneath him, I cradled his head with my other hand, the life already fading from his eyes.

"Ace—" Blood gurgled from his mouth.

My chest cracked open with deep agony. "Oh, God, Ben! No, I'm so sorry! Please don't die, don't go, don't leave me again!"

His massive body slowly slid from my grasp, and I melted to the ground with him. The only person who could help him was unconscious.

He stared deeply into my eyes. "It makes sense now...."

"What does?" I whipped my head to the others. "Get The Keepers! Maybe they can help him!"

He gurgled more blood and managed to spit it to the side. "The connection." Another cough. I wiped his mouth with my sleeve, and tears dripped onto his face. "To Dianna. It was never love, it was never about her and me." He choked up another fresh gush of blood. Eric must have punctured his stomach. Ben reached up with a shaky hand and slid it over my arm, up to my face, where he held my cheek in his palm. "It was always you." His smile made my heart wring. "Time just wasn't on our side."

"But it is," I replied and kissed his palm. "It is, Ben. I swear. It just takes a while for you to catch up."

His pain-filled eyes watered over. "All this time...are we...the future..."

Behind me, I could hear the others tying up Eric's un-conscious body, but all I could see was Ben. The world blackened around the edges of my vision, and only he and I were in the sand. I just nodded, pressing my lips together as the crack between them filled with tears.

"We're together in the future," I told him, and he looked so happy, despite the blood and the life draining from his eyes. "We found each other without knowing who the other even was."

He tried to stifle the next spurt of blood that crawled up his throat, tears spilling over. "I…found my place?"

I put my hand over his, where he still cradled my face. "Yes," I managed to say, but it was barely a whisper. "With me."

I held him as he took his last breath, and those warm brown eyes I loved so much turned lifeless and empty. I buried my face in his chest and sobbed, the anguish building and building within me. A guttural, fierce scream ripped from my chest as I shot a look to the skies, letting it erupt.

The Cobham women were cursed to an eternity of heartbreak and loss. I couldn't live like this. I couldn't go back and face a future without Ben, a future where the few people I loved still remained.

Footsteps crunched in the distance, and I turned my head to find The Keepers approaching. My heart sped up.

"Please!" I begged them. "Please, help him!"

One of them went to where Lottie and Kiri held Eric on the ground while another removed the magic ties that bound Finn. Their leader came to me and knelt at my side with a saddened look in her eyes. Silently, she smoothed over Ben's already paling skin.

"He's gone," was all she said.

"*Bring him back.*" Desperations raked under my skin.

She shook her head. "Benjamin Cook does not possess a soul."

Because he'd traded it to save my mother.

My arms struggled to hold his dead weight, but I pulled him as close as possible, sobbing into his neck. The air around us tightened, and The Keeper touched my back gently.

"Audrey Cobham," she said solemnly. "It's time for you to go home."

She'd opened a portal, and on the other side…my childhood home. The beach I was taken from just weeks ago. I whipped a look at her, panic pulling at my face.

"No!" I shook my head. "No, I'm not ready to go! I can't–he won't be there!"

She sighed thoughtfully and exchanged a glance with her sisters. "I'm sorry that we cannot help with this matter of life and death." She slowly looked toward the sea and gave me a tender smile. "But there are those of us who deal in wishes."

My mouth gaped. "I…I'd asked the sirens for a wish. They refused."

"But are you not a siren yourself?"

Hope blossomed in my chest, just enough to taste, and my eyes searched hers for the answer I needed. Could I do it? Was I able to pull a wish pearl from the sea?

"I wanted to extend my condolences for your grand-mother's passing," she said, stretching to her feet as she peered down at me. "Constance was like a daughter to us."

That's right. I'd almost forgotten that my grandmother was once raised by The Keepers, just as Eric was. It was how she learned of time travel in the first place.

She walked over to her sisters, who held Eric's sagging body between them and nodded at Lottie and Finn, who returned the respectful gesture. Kiri stood off to the side, no longer wrought with confusion but watching with awe and admiration.

The lead Keeper stopped one last time and glanced at me. "Say hello to Henry and Dianna for me, will you?"

There. That was the answer I needed. She knew I wasn't leaving without Ben alive. She smiled, and another por-tal opened next to the one reserved for me. The three of them stepped through, taking Eric with them.

"Lass," Finn said carefully and stomped over to where I sat crumpled in the sand with Ben in my lap. "Go, do what ye need to do. I got him."

I hadn't realized how tightly I gripped Ben's body until I told my fingers to let go. My hands throbbed as I allowed Finn to relieve me of the weight. I scrambled over to the water's edge and stared at it, trying to recall the memory of the mother siren and how she'd so effortlessly scooped her hand through the water and pulled out pearls.

I just needed one.

Shakily, I submerged my hand and let it sit there momentarily as I focused every possible thought on wishes and pearls, silently searching for that spark of magic that lived in the recesses of my gut. I felt them like balls of jelly between my fingers. But my hand came out empty.

"Damn it!" I sobbed angrily and tried again. I slapped at the water and howled with frustration.

Lottie crouched down beside me. "Audrey."

My head snapped up. It was the first time she acknowledged who I was.

"Just go home," she said. "Go back to your family where it's safe, and be thankful you're alive."

I shook my head. "No, I won't go without him. If he dies here, who knows what happens to future Ben?" I stared at her. "You'd do it for Gus."

She couldn't argue with me.

I swooped my hand through the water again, my stomach solid with determination. I felt them brush against my fingers and focused as I scooped them from the sea. Four wish pearls, each a varying shade and shimmer of white.

I cried at the relief.

"Can you give your mother a message for me?" Lottie asked.

My heart nearly stopped. "Of course."

She smiled to herself. "Tell her…tell her, thank you." I

could see a sort of weight lift from her shoulders.

"That's it? Just *thank you*?"

"She'll know what you mean."

I rolled the pearls in my hand and handed one to her. She looked at me, aghast. "Use it how you see fit. Brings Gus back. Get rich. It doesn't matter. But find happiness."

"Audrey…" Her eyes glistened as she pinched it between her fingers.

"I grew up hearing so many wonderful stories about you guys. You're my family, even if you barely know me."

She smiled, the first genuine expression I'd seen her make this entire time. "We know you."

She helped me to my feet, and we walked over to where Finn and Kiri waited quietly on a bank. I handed Kiri the second pearl. "This will grant you any wish you want." Her eyes bulged, and she looked to Finn and Lottie for reassuring nods. "Just throw it in the water and say your wish before it dissolves. Find your brother, Kiri. Get him back."

She leaped from the grass and wrapped her arms around me. "Thank you, Ace. Or should I say, Audrey?"

"I should be thanking you. I couldn't have done this without you." I pulled away with a laugh. "I'm so sorry for getting you mixed up in this mess. But I'm glad we met."

Her cheeks warmed. "Me, too."

I glanced down at Finn, who gleamed up at me with the glow of a proud uncle. "Ye best be getting' on yer way, lass."

I smiled and handed him a third pearl. "Thank you for all you did for me, but also for my mother. She loves you dearly, you know."

"Aye," he paused, tearing up. He shook it off and made a show of rolling his eyes. "Tell yer ma I miss her buns."

I stood between him and Lottie. "Can I ask one last favor?"

Of course—anything, their voices overlapped.

I walked over and picked up the jar of Maria's ashes, and handed it to Finn. "Make sure this goes somewhere that no one will find."

"I swear it." He tucked it under his arm.

I turned to Lottie. "And my favor from you." I placed my last pearl in her hand. "I need you to wish for Ben to live. For his wound to heal and for him to forget my true identity."

"Why not do it yourself?"

"I'm not sure if I can use my own pearls," I replied and shrugged. "I'm still fuzzy on the rules. I just don't...want to waste it."

She clenched her fist and held it to her chest. "Understood."

I glanced at the portal. "It's best I leave before he comes to. Just tell him...tell him I left with The Keepers."

I knew he'd be heartbroken. My sweet, soft, rugged

man. He was like an old teddy bear. But a clean break would be best because I wasn't sure of my ability to say no to Ben in any time. I could hardly admit it, but I could be swayed to stay. And I knew I had to go home, not just for myself, but for my family.

With a deep breath, I stepped one leg through the portal and turned one last time to wave goodbye. I leaned all the way in, and it closed behind me, leaving me on the balmy seaside beach behind my grandmother's house. My house. An air of familiarity hung in the air.

No, it couldn't be.

I raced into the house and scanned everything, but the digital calendar clock in the kitchen made me melt with relief.

It was the same night I left. It was as if I wasn't gone at all. I bolted upstairs, holding a breath in my lungs. It burned in my chest as I barged through the bedroom door, and Ben rolled over with alarm. Through the window that faced the sea, the faintest sliver of light touched the horizon. Morning would be here soon.

"Ace?" Ben croaked and peeled the blanket back.

I fell to my knees with a long wailing sob. I did it. I made it back. My body crumpled in on itself, and I cried harder than ever. All the weight of exhaustion, fear, and stress from the last few weeks just erupted from me, and Ben waited, almost as if he knew.

When the tears dried up and I could breathe, he came near. I felt his hand splay over my back, and I rose to look in his face. I expected pure shock, but I only found a sleepy smile.

"You know," he said, purposely ignoring my breakdown to distract me. "I had the craziest dream about you." He paused and leaned back, looking me up and down. "Although, I'm starting to think it wasn't a dream."

I shrugged off my heavy, dirty leather coat and everything I carried and crawled to him. I collapsed into his warm, bare chest and rested my head in the crook of his shoulder and neck. His arms draped over me, holding me close as he kissed my forehead. For him, a few hours had gone by.

I brushed the tip of my finger over the nasty white scar on his side, one I surely would have noticed the night we first made love right here in this room. His whole body tensed, and his arms tightened, pulling me even closer to him. He must have realized it truly was a memory.

"It wasn't a dream, was it?"

My eyes stung, and I shook my head. "No."

I watched as the last three hundred years replied in his eyes, but differently now, with the memory of who I really was.

"It was you all along?"

"Yes." I put my forehead to his. "I love you,

Benjamin Cook."

"Fuck, I love how you say my name."

His body vibrated with a moan as I leaned into him. I had weeks of pirate grime stuck to me, but he didn't seem to care. He took my mouth in an all-encompassing kiss that screamed one word. *Mine.* He devoured my lips as his hand wrung through my hair. And when he finally broke us free, I gasped for air.

"I love you, too, Ace."

Or chests heaved together as something seemed to lift from us, seeping from our blood like a light gas, evaporating into the air.

The curse on our bloodlines. It was broken.

"You know," Ben said coyly, running a hand up my thigh. "We're both immortal."

"Correct," I replied with a waiting grin.

He held my face and stared into my eyes. "To the end of time, then?"

I paused, my lips just a hair from his. "To the end of time."

THE END

"A Time Travel Series to Give Outlander a Run For its Money!"

★★★★★ – InDTale Magazine

And if you love the **high stakes danger, magic,**
and **epic fated romance** of this spin off
A Curse of the Blood Pearl then you'll devour
Candace's original **Time Travel Fantasy
Series Dark Tides.**

Can Dianna charm the crew of **The Devil's Heart**
before they kill her ancestors, or will she just fall
deeper under the captain's spell?

ABOUT THE AUTHOR

Candace Osmond is a **#1 International** &

USA TODAY Bestselling Author of Fantasy Romance.

She's also an Award-Winning Screenwriter.

She currently resides on the rocky East Coast of

Canada with her husband, two kids, and bulldog.

Connect with Candace online! She **LOVES** to hear

from readers!